TANGO TROUBLE

A MAGICAL MANE MYSTERY

STELLA BIXBY

This novel is a work of fiction. Names, characters, places, and incidents are either a product of the author's imagination or are used fictitiously. Any resemblance to actual persons, living or dead, businesses, events, or locales is entirely coincidental.

Copyright © 2021 by Crystal S. Ferry

All rights reserved.

No part of this book may be reproduced or transmitted in any form or by any means, electronic or mechanical, including photocopying, recording, or by any information storage and retrieval system presently available or yet to be invented without permission in writing from the publisher, except for the use of brief quotations in a book review.

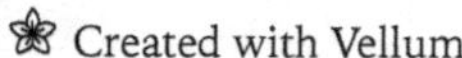 Created with Vellum

For Shawna—my write or die, gif queen, textie bestie, lover of love, Enneagram Guru, friend for life.
Thank you a million times over.

"Reach, lift, pull, and down," I said.

The woman next to me groaned.

"You've got this," I said. "I know it's heavy, but we have to get this move executed so you can get it on a conveyor belt."

She reached for the handle of the suitcase and tugged, but she couldn't quite get it off the step it was on.

"Come on," I said. "You can do it. Pull. You're almost there."

She gave the bag a quick yank, and it nearly toppled her over.

I put out a hand to steady her, but she didn't need it. She righted herself and looked up at me, beaming.

"You did it!" I practically jumped up and down in excitement.

Renée let go of the handle and dropped her arms to her sides. "Whew, that was hard."

"You've made serious progress," I said. "Before you know it, you'll be on your way to Argentina."

"Once I get this mastered, I'll just have to work on lifting my luggage to the rack on the plane." Renée wiped sweat from her wrinkled forehead. She had short white hair and the eyes of a grandmother—kind and caring.

At least, I assumed that's what a grandmother's eyes would look like. I'd never met my grandmother.

"One step at a time," I said. "I'm sure if you asked, Clancy would lift your carry-on for you."

"I can't go letting him think I need him." By the way she smiled, I knew she was only partially kidding. She was determined to be self-sufficient. "Let's take a break and get some celebratory hot cocoa."

I followed Renée further into the house.

Or rather—mansion.

Renée and Clancy had just moved back to town after winning the lottery or a jackpot or something. Renée had grown up on the farm they currently lived on. She'd made quick work demolishing the old farmhouse and building a mansion that looked like it belonged somewhere far more modern than rural Cliff Haven, Iowa.

"Jasmine? Would you be a dear and make us two mugs of the special cocoa I whipped up the other day?" Renée asked the woman who acted as her personal assistant.

Jasmine—a pretty woman in her early twenties—nodded and started making herself busy in the kitchen.

"Would you like a glass of water?" Renée asked me. "Your workouts always leave me parched."

"I'm okay, but thanks." I glanced around at the beautiful kitchen that led into the dining room and living room.

"Oh shoot," Renée said as ice spilled out of the refrigerator door onto the floor. "Jasmine, would you please clean that up? And call the repairman to fix that stupid ice machine? I keep forgetting it does that."

Jasmine left the mugs of cocoa she was doctoring to clean up the floor.

"Thank you," Renée said, filling her glass with water. "We'll be by the fireplace if you don't mind bringing the hot cocoa in there."

"Of course," Jasmine said with a smile.

"Is Clancy getting excited about the trip?" I asked, sitting in one of the wing-backed chairs next to a large glass fireplace.

"You know Clancy." Renée fiddled with a small paw print charm on a chain around her neck. "He's a pain in my batoot. He keeps asking if we can just go to Florida or Texas."

"Is he opposed to leaving the country?"

"I think it's more that he doesn't want to leave his precious casino." She rolled her eyes. "Though I suppose I should be thankful for that casino right about now."

I glanced around at the open-concept home. A loft extended above us, leading to bedrooms on either side. Large windows overlooked the snowy field that would likely produce corn in the coming months.

A chime sounded near the sliding glass door leading to the porch.

Renée sat up taller to see, then slouched back down. "That stupid sensor," she said. "Clancy is so paranoid someone will try to take everything from us. He installed sensors all over the house to warn us when someone is at the door. The problem is, they go off for every little thing. A bird, a bug, the shifting light. It drives me mad."

"Your hot cocoa," Jasmine said, bringing a tray of beverages to the table between us.

"Thank you," Renée and I said in unison.

She nodded and walked back to the kitchen.

"I still haven't gotten used to someone doing everything for me," Renée said, then took a sip of the cocoa.

I sipped mine and let the perfectly warm and creamy deliciousness slide down my throat and into my stomach. Tingles reached up my neck and into my scalp.

"Ooh, I think Ellie likes the cocoa," Renée shouted over her shoulder at Jasmine, pointing at my head.

I pulled my ponytail around to find my hair a soft shade of pink with shimmery golden strands.

"I wish my hair would do fun things like that," Renée said, then leaned in closer. "I also wish I was a witch."

I'd recently stopped correcting people when they called me a witch. I'd grown up in foster homes, only staying as long as my hair behaved. The minute I lost control of my emotions, my hair would change, and I'd be back to square one with a new family.

Because of that, I'd done everything in my ability to keep my hair—and my magic—under control. Which had basically stunted it. I was slowly learning to use my magic and coax it out of hiding.

"Speaking of magic," I said. "This hot cocoa is truly phenomenal."

"You think?" Renée asked. "It's my mother's secret recipe. People would kill for that recipe."

The thought of someone killing over a recipe would

have shocked me before moving to Cliff Haven. Now, it seemed like people would kill for less.

"Let's hope it doesn't come to that," I said.

She burst out in a boisterous laugh. "I was kidding."

I laughed along with her. Maybe I'd seen too much murder in the last few months.

The chime rang again.

Renée stood and walked to the door. I followed.

She was right. There was absolutely no reason for the chime to go off.

"It was probably a bug." She sighed. "Or maybe a ghost."

A bug was probably less likely than a ghost at the below-freezing temps outside. It had been so cold for so long, I was starting to wonder why people lived here in the winter. I'd grown up in Colorado where the winters were snow-covered but also semi-warm. Iowa winters were miserably cold.

"I should head out," I said, finishing my hot cocoa. "I'll see you in a couple of days. We can work on your overhead bin skills."

"You know, there's something else I'd like to learn," Renée said, following me to the front door, where my shoes and magical jacket waited for me. The first time I'd come for a session with Renée, she insisted I take off my shoes. Not because of the dirt, but because the floors were extra slick when wet, and she didn't want me to fall.

"What else would you like to learn?" I asked.

"To tango. Clancy said if I could find a dance class, he'd go with me. I'm sure he said that because he thought there was no chance I'd find a class, but maybe you could do one?"

I'd learned a bit about ballroom dancing in college. And I had the perfect venue in my renovated barn. "Let me throw the idea out to the others, and I'll let you know."

"Wonderful," Renée said, clapping her hands together.

I'd parked Mona—my VW Microbus—where the sun would keep her warm and prayed she would start with the below-freezing temps.

On the other side of Mona was Clancy's shiny new sports car. His voice was muffled from inside, but it sounded like he was yelling at someone.

I'd often wondered why Clancy and Renée were even together. She was such a sweetheart, and he was so slimy. He was the type that knew everything about everyone even though he hadn't grown up around town. He'd somehow finagled his way into the group of old farmers who regularly inhabited a table at the local café, which wasn't easy to do as they were a relatively tight bunch.

I didn't work at the café much anymore since my traveling therapeutic recreation business became more successful, but when I had, it seemed like they all got along okay.

As I slid into Mona's driver's seat, Clancy opened his door and shouted, "Remember who you're talking to. I'm the boss." He slammed the car door and then looked at me.

Heat ran from my hair follicles to my fingertips. If I had to guess, my hair was turning red. Which usually indicated danger.

I waved at Clancy, hoping he'd simply go inside with a wave.

But I wasn't so lucky.

He narrowed his eyes and marched right over to my door.

"What's this I hear about you filling my wife's head with ideas of leaving the country?"

"I-I didn't—"

"How many other old ladies have you scammed? Telling them the only way they can travel is if they take your exercise programs?"

My hair could have been on fire, it burned so intensely. "I would never—"

"I know all the tricks of the trade," he interrupted. "Renée is a sweet woman who will believe anything anyone tells her. But I won't stand for her throwing our hard-earned money down the drain for someone to teach her how to pick up a suitcase."

"It's called range of motion," I said. "As you age, you can lose the ability to do things like that."

He pointed a finger at my face, so close he was almost touching my nose. "Don't try your hocus-pocus on me. Your hair is a nifty trick, but I'm not so easily brain-washed. As of this moment, you're fired. Don't bother coming back."

"Clancy," Renée's voice came from the front door. "What in the world are you hollering about?" She marched down the stairs in her house slippers and out into the snowy driveway toward us.

"I don't want you working out with this woman

anymore." Clancy's voice was slightly less intimidating. "You know darn well how to lift a suitcase."

"Thanks to Ellie, I can now," Renée said. "Before she started working with me, I was a weak old woman. Now, I feel wonderful."

"Good, because I just fired her." Clancy crossed his arms over his chest.

"You did what?" Renée's voice lowered to a whisper. I'd never seen her so fierce. Even Clancy cowered a bit.

"It's a waste of our money," Clancy whined.

"We have more money than we know what to do with," Renée hissed. "And you do not get to dictate how I spend my portion. Heck, you could use some of Ellie's classes yourself. You can't even bend down to tie your own shoelaces."

Clancy's face was a shade of red that might have rivaled my hair color.

"It'll be a cold day in the Devil's land before I take classes from her." He threw his hands in the air. "If you want to waste your portion of the money on some money-grubbing witch, be my guest. But I won't be going to Argentina with you. Maybe you can take your new friend here. I'm sure she'd love a free trip."

He stormed away.

Renée and I watched as he climbed the steps, slipping on the top one, before slamming the front door behind him.

She turned back to me and smiled. "I'm sorry about him. He's just cranky because of the farming deal."

"Farming deal?" I asked, trying to get my heart rate to slow.

"We have all this property to farm, but we have no equipment or know-how. We're trying to find a farmer who will do it for us so we can make some passive income. But, as you can see, Clancy isn't easy to please. He wants the best deal possible, and he's not willing to settle for anything less."

"I see. I'm sorry about causing trouble. I had no intention of—"

"Stop right there, young lady." Renée reached out and touched my shoulder. "Clancy is a grumpy old man, but he has a soft spot for me. He'll come around about Argentina."

"Do you still want to do the dance classes? He might not want to come if he knows I'm the instructor."

"Oh, he'll come. He promised." She winked. "Text me when you get home, so I know you didn't slide into a ditch."

"Will do," I said.

She turned back to the house, leaving me with an angry shade of red hair, a heart beating uncontrollably, and an uneasiness in my gut.

2

———

Penelope bolted toward me when I got home and made my way from the garage—where I parked Mona—to the barn studio. If I was going to propose doing dance classes, I needed to assess the space to make sure it was suitable first.

"Hello, my sweet girl," I said, gathering the squirming piggy into my arms. She wiggled her nose against my cheek in what I thought of her version of a kiss. "How was your morning?"

She let out an enthusiastic oink.

"That good, huh?" I laughed and set her back on the ground.

She followed me into the barn. As I flipped on the lights, I exhaled.

This was my happy place.

The overhead lights illuminated what used to be a dirt floor but was now a beautiful wood. The memory of the entire town coming together to help me create the studio of my dreams sometimes snuck up on me, bringing on all sorts of warm, fuzzy feelings.

Here, I'd found my home. I was surrounded by people who loved me and accepted me—magic and all. Even if they weren't related to me by blood, they were my family.

Penelope oinked, letting me know my hair was changing colors.

I swished it over my shoulder to find it a soft pink.

It was funny how pink and red were so close to the same shade yet so far apart in terms of my hair's moods. Where pink meant happy, red warned of danger.

"What do you think about dance classes?" I asked Penelope, who was actively spinning in circles in the middle of the floor as if she had known exactly what I was thinking. "Maybe you could help me teach them."

"I'd like to see that," a voice said behind me.

I whipped around to find Xander leaning against the door frame with a gorgeous grin on his face.

I looked away.

I'd fallen into that trap before. He'd been pretty clear about us only being friends.

"I think Penelope could give me a run for my money with those dance moves," I said as Penelope spun one last circle, then charged to Xander, who picked her up and gave her a quick squeeze.

"Dance classes, huh?" Xander said, lowering Penelope back to the ground.

"A client asked if I could teach her to tango. She wants to go to Argentina. We've been working on range of motion and strength for her airplane ride."

Xander walked into the studio, wiping his leather boots on the rug before stepping on the hardwood. He was your typical bad boy in looks—tight jeans, leather jacket, shoulder-length hair. But even being a warlock—a man with magic—he wasn't as rough and tumble as he seemed.

"Before I met you, I didn't know there was such a thing as therapeutic recreation."

"Please don't tell me you think it's a hoax too. I've had enough criticism for one day."

Xander's eyebrows pushed together, wrinkling his forehead. "I'd never say that. I've seen the results of your business. They would be incredible even if you didn't have magic on your side."

I still wasn't sure how the magic in me worked when it came to my clients. But I had seen faster improvements than seemed possible in many of them.

"Who questioned your business?" Xander asked. His tone was an attempt at lighthearted, but I could tell he was on the defensive.

"It's not a big deal," I said. "Not everyone has to buy into it."

If he knew Clancy had tried to fire me, he would likely be in Clancy's driveway demanding an apology. I'd told him more times than I could count that I didn't need someone protecting me. I'd taken care of myself for so many years without the help of a man or anyone else. But Xander had protection running through his veins. It made me wonder whether he had sisters or something, but he never talked about himself or his family. Even though I'd call him one of my closest friends, I knew practically nothing about him. It was infuriating at times.

"If you're having problems with someone—"

I held up a hand and shook my head. "I'm fine. Not everyone has to believe in my methods."

He looked like he wanted to say more but thought better of it. "So about those dance classes?"

My thoughts returned to their original topic—the studio. "I was trying to determine whether the space is big enough to do them here."

Xander shoved his hands in his pockets and leaned back on his heels. "Do you want my two cents?"

"Sure," I said slowly.

He took a step toward the back of the barn, where I kept most of the equipment and a hanging curtain that divided the front of the barn from the very back. "If you move a few of these benches and chairs and put the exercise balls up in a net off the floor, I think you'd have plenty of space for at least a few couples."

"I agree," I said. "For the moment, I could move them behind the curtain. It would make it tight back there for a while, but Penelope and I could get over that."

"Speaking of behind the curtain, anything new?"

He was referencing the magical mural my mother had painted before she fled town to have me under a veil of secrecy. She then left me at a fire station and disappeared forever. "Nothing."

"Like nothing out of the ordinary or—"

"Nothing at all." I sighed. "Since Harriet left, there hasn't been a single person in the painting."

If you didn't count my mother, Harriet was my only known living relative—a cousin—who had recently exited my life just as abruptly as she'd entered.

"That's strange," he said.

I shrugged. "We'll see." I couldn't let him see how badly it hurt that my mother's mural hadn't changed. In fact, if I was correct, it almost seemed to be fading somehow. The scene of the farm—the farm I'd inherited from my grandmother—was the same. Barn, corn, trees. But the colors didn't seem as vibrant as usual. Maybe when there were people in the painting, they livened it up. Or maybe I was looking too hard for a change.

"About those dance lessons," Xander said.

I glanced at him, standing there with a grin on his face. "What?"

"I've been known to dance a bit in my life."

"You dance?" I couldn't keep the astonishment out of my voice.

"My father insisted I learn."

My heart leaped at the mention of his father. He'd never talked about his family before. I turned away from him, took a breath, and tried to think about something else. The same way I used to when I was a child trying to keep my hair from changing.

"Are you offering to help me teach the classes?" I asked, scooping Penelope into my arms as she let out a low oink that told me my hair was changing regardless of my attempts to keep it under control.

His boots on the wood floor echoed in the silence as he came closer to me. We'd kissed once. A kiss that had burned itself into my memory and often ignited my dreams.

The thought of dancing with him sent magical sparks up my neck and into my scalp. There was no use trying to keep my hair from changing at this point. I could see it turning a shimmery gold and twisting into ringlets out of the corner of my eye.

Surely my cheeks were an embarrassing shade of pink, but I had no choice but to face him when his hands landed on my shoulders, and he spun me around. Sparks seemed to flow from his fingertips throughout my body.

"It could be fun." He looked down at me, his voice a low rumble.

"Then it's a deal," I said, though my voice cracked a bit. Every part of me wanted to kiss him. And from the look on his face, he was thinking the same thing.

Would it be so bad to date a warlock? I'd been warned that warlocks weren't always the most upstanding people. But Xander made it a point to never lie to me. He may not have told me everything I wanted to know, but he was honest about his secrecy.

And he smelled so good.

Just one little kiss wouldn't hurt.

I raised a bit, bringing my heels off the floor.

Then all heck broke loose.

Penelope let out a squeal that nearly made me drop her.

She snapped out at Xander's arm.

He pulled it back in time to avoid being bitten by her sharp piggy teeth.

"Whoa," Xander said.

"Penelope!" I was holding onto her for dear life as she wiggled with so much force I thought I might drop her. And if I dropped her, her twig-like legs could snap.

"Hold on," I said. "Stop wiggling." I squatted down

and put her on the floor, where she planted her feet square between Xander and me, her snout pointing up at him as if in warning.

Xander chuckled and ran a hand through his hair. "Sorry, Penelope."

Why was he apologizing to her? She was being ridiculous. "What has gotten into you?" I sat on the floor and put a hand on her back. She still didn't turn to look at me.

Xander crouched down but didn't dare reach out to touch her as she stood in her guarded position. "Just dancing," he whispered. "That's it."

My chest tightened. Once again, I'd gotten too worked up over my *friend*. How many times did he have to tell me we were just friends before I'd get it through my head? He couldn't help that every time we touched, electricity flowed through me. It would make dancing with him a challenge, but it was doable.

I nodded once. "Just dancing."

Penelope's muscles loosened, and she came to curl up in my lap, her gaze still fixed on Xander.

"I'm going to take off," Xander said, standing. "Just let me know when these dance classes are going to take place. I'll be here."

I smiled. "Thanks."

He smiled back, and the tightness in my chest eased a bit.

Penelope let out a low grumble, almost like a growl.

Xander must not have heard it over his footsteps as he walked out into the cold.

"What is the matter with you?" I asked when I could be relatively certain Xander was out of earshot. "Xander is a good man—a warlock, yes—but a good one. He's done nothing but good for us."

Penelope grumbled a bit more and rested her head on my leg. I leaned forward and cuddled into her. "It's okay. We're just going to dance."

3

The smell of pancakes and coffee filled my nose as the jingle bells on the door rang when I walked into Katie's Café bright and early the next day.

"Think you can remember how to take an order?" Bex teased as I tied on my black server apron.

"I'll do my best."

Bex was my best human friend in Cliff Haven.

Scratch that.

Bex was my best human friend in the world.

Since the moment I walked into the café, nervous about getting a job, she had taken me under her wing. We'd been close ever since. Today, Bex wore her trademark bellbottom jeans with a flowy pink top. Her deep black hair was in multiple braids, fastened by a loose scrunchie at the back of her neck.

The local farmers were the only customers to have arrived, and Bex had already filled their coffee and taken their orders.

"How's Miss Ellie today?" Earl asked. When I'd first met him, he was a grumbly old man. Now, he was still a grumbly old man, but with a soft spot for me.

"Doing well," I said. "And how are you?"

"Feeling great." Earl twisted in his seat. "Those sessions really worked out the kinks in my back."

"I'm happy to hear it," I said.

"Speaking of," Hank said, his jolly red cheeks lifting in a smile. "I tweaked my knee on the ice the other day. The doctor wants to give me meds to shut me up, but I thought maybe you could help?"

"I'm happy to take a look," I said.

"Don't tell me you've bought into her lies too," a man said behind me.

I turned to find Clancy walking to the table, a newspaper under his arm, and a snide grin on his face.

"What are you going on about?" Earl challenged.

"She's got my wife in a frenzy about going to Argentina," Clancy said. "But only if she can do everything on her own. Lift her own bags, buckle her own seatbelt, blah, blah, blah."

"Those sound like perfectly reasonable things for someone to do on their own," Bex said, coming to stand beside me.

Clancy grunted. "Sounds like she has you brainwashed, too. Did she use her magical hair witch powers on the entire town?"

Earl sighed and stood, towering over Clancy. "We've been nothing but friendly to you since you came to town, Clancy. But Ellie is family, and we won't stand for you talking about her in such a manner."

Clancy glanced around at the other farmers, who stared right back at him, nodding in agreement with Earl. Bex wrapped a protective arm around my shoulder.

"I knew we should have moved somewhere else," Clancy said. "But Renée just had to live on her family farm. Well, I'm done."

He threw the paper on the table and stormed out of the café, forcing the couple entering to dodge out of his path.

Earl sat back down and continued drinking his coffee as if nothing had happened.

Bex squeezed my shoulder and left to take the couple's order.

Another man walked in a few seconds after. I waited for him to choose a table before I took him a menu. But, much to my surprise, he plopped down in the chair Clancy had been about to sit in. Right next to Earl.

A couple of the farmers nodded their hellos.

I looked again, but I'd never seen this man before. I hadn't been working as much at the café, but I was getting pretty good at recognizing the faces from around town.

I slid a menu in front of him and asked, "Can I get you something to drink?"

He smiled and removed his stocking cap, revealing gray hair that stuck up all over his head. "I'll take a coffee, black, please."

"Ellie, this is Weston Peters," Earl said. "He's not usually around this time of year."

"I came back early to pick up a few more farms," Weston said as I poured him a steaming mug of aromatic coffee.

"What do you mean, pick up a few more farms?" I was still figuring things out when it came to farming.

"I rent fields other people don't want to farm themselves. I have the equipment, they have the land. It works really well." Weston spoke with a warm, confident tone.

"That's interesting. How many fields do you farm?" This sounded exactly like what Clancy and Renée were looking for.

"Right now, none," he said. "Last spring, my biggest farm sold to a developer right before planting. I was out a lot of money. That's why I'm here early—to try and land another big one."

Earl glanced over the top of the paper at Weston. "He won't go for it when he finds out who you are."

I thought I saw Weston's cheeks redden a bit as he turned to face Earl. "It's been so many years. I don't know why it would matter."

I wanted to tell Weston about Renée and Clancy's farm but didn't want to interrupt.

"I'll put in Weston's usual order if you want to get him," Bex nodded to the handsome man coming through the front door, then winked at me.

When he and I made eye contact, he smiled. I couldn't help but smile back. He was probably six-foot-tall, wore a hoodie and khakis, and had gelled blond hair.

I walked over and handed him a menu.

"Can I get you anything? Coffee maybe? We have the best crispy-edged pancakes in the entire world." I was flirting, but I couldn't help it. It wasn't every day a cute guy came to Cliff Haven.

"In the entire world, huh?" He handed the unopened

menu back to me. "I'll take a stack, some bacon, and black coffee, please."

"Sure thing," I said. "I'll be right back with the coffee."

I put his order in with the kitchen and returned with a steaming mug of coffee. "Here's that coffee for you."

He looked up from the open file he had in front of him. "Have you lived here long?"

"Not really," I said. "Less than a year. Why?"

"I wanted to know if you've met anyone who goes by the name Baby Bear."

I almost laughed but realized he wasn't kidding. "As in an adult?"

He nodded.

"I can't say that I have." I looked back at where Bex was chatting with Jasmine, who was probably there to pick up food for Clancy since he stormed out before being waited upon. "A friend of mine has lived here longer than me, though. And those farmers have lived here practically their entire lives. I could ask one of them."

He shook his head. "That's okay. I need my business to stay confidential. You just looked trustworthy."

"I like to think I am," I said. "What kind of business are you in?"

He lowered his voice. "I'm a private investigator."

"Is that so?" I asked. "Private investigators are basically cops, right?"

"Without the badge, gun, and taxpayer dollars." He sipped his coffee. "I'm typically hired by individuals who want me to look into something—cheating spouse, fraudulent insurance claims, those sorts of things."

"So you think this Baby Bear is a cheating spouse?"

He raised an eyebrow. "That's confidential."

"Right," I said as the bell from the kitchen rang. "It sounds like your food is ready. I'll be right back."

But when I got back, he was gone. On the table, he left fifty dollars and a note that said—*rain check on the cakes.*

4

The early morning women's fitness club met a few times a week in my studio. In the winter, we did yoga or chair aerobics. When the weather warmed up, we'd walk outside.

Katie, as usual, was the first to walk through the door. She shrugged off her bright pink, fur-lined winter jacket with matching hat, scarf, and gloves revealing gray leopard print tights and an oversized black sweater that hung off one shoulder. Her outfit was something a young woman— like her actress daughter—would wear. But Katie was well past her youth, as were all of my regular morning group clients.

"Good morning, sunshine," Katie said, kissing me on the cheek and taking the mug of coffee from my hands. I'd recently set up a coffee bar right in the studio, so we didn't have to walk between the house and the barn in the cold.

"How are you this morning?" I asked.

"Stiff," Katie admitted. "I am sick and tired of this weather. I miss flowers and green grass and warmth."

"You're telling me," Fran said, walking in with Amy. They were quite the couple—Fran in her regular outfit of no-nonsense jeans and a plaid button-down shirt, and Amy with bright bubblegum pink hair and a metal band t-shirt. "This weather is a serious downer."

"I think I have an idea to cheer it up a bit," I said, handing Fran and Amy their coffees. "But I want to wait until the others are here to talk about it."

"Ooh, I like new ideas," Amy said with a wink. "The coffee is extra yummy this morning."

She told me that at least once a week, even though I made the coffee the same way every single day.

Bonnie walked through the door, shortly followed by Nancy. The two of them could not have been more different in appearance. Bonnie was tall and dressed like she was heading to a fitness class in Los Angeles or New York City, whereas Nancy was a tattooed version of Mrs. Claus with her rosy cheeks, white hair, and propensity to wear red.

"Okay, we're all here," Amy said. "Spill."

Bonnie and Nancy took their coffees from my hands with words of greeting and thanks.

"I was at Renée Wright's house a couple of days ago, and she mentioned wanting to learn the tango." I took a breath. "I wanted to see what you all thought about doing some dance lessons."

Excitement spread across their faces, and they all started talking at once like a group of teenage girls who had just been told they'd made the varsity cheerleading team.

"I'll take that as a yes?" I said, trying to speak over them.

"Oh definitely," Nancy said. "Hank and I love to dance."

"Do you think Earl will go for it?" I asked Katie.

"Earl would do anything for you," Katie said.

Even Bonnie, who wasn't married, seemed excited. "Do we have to come as a couple, or would singles be allowed?"

"Singles would definitely be allowed," I said. "Does anyone know if Weston Peters is single? He seems like a nice man."

Katie laughed. "He's single all right, but he won't go for Bonnie." She looked at Bonnie. "No offense."

"None taken," Bonnie said. Bonnie and Katie hadn't always seen eye to eye, but recently they'd become closer friends.

"Why wouldn't he go for Bonnie?" I asked.

"He's still hung up on an old relationship," Katie said. "But that doesn't mean he wouldn't make a good dance partner."

"Then it's settled. How about we have the first class this Saturday evening?"

They all agreed, and we started our morning yoga practice. Now, I just had to brush up on my tango skills.

When I pulled into Renée's driveway, a shiny blue pickup truck sat where I usually parked Mona. I pulled up next to it, close enough that if Clancy came home, he could still drive up to the garages.

Jasmine let me in and escorted me to where Renée sat drinking coffee, a huge smile on her face. When she met my gaze, she blushed. "Ellie, you're here."

I glanced at my phone to make sure I wasn't too early.

"No, no," she said. "You're right on time. I'm afraid I lost track of time with an old friend."

She motioned to someone sitting just beyond my view. When he stood and turned around the corner, he smiled. "Ellie and I have met," Weston said.

The pieces clicked in my mind. Renée must have been the woman Weston was hung up on, and that's why Earl told Weston he wouldn't get the farm contract.

"It's nice to see you again," I said.

"I should go anyway," Weston said, turning back to Renée. "I've taken up enough of your day. But do think about what I said."

Renée smiled, her face brightening. "I don't think it'll be a problem at all."

"Well, talk to Clancy first." He lifted her hand to his lips and kissed it gently. "It's been nice catching up."

Her cheeks were a deep red. "Do stop by again."

He nodded at me as he walked by toward the door. "Nice seeing you too."

I smiled, then turned back to Renée. When Weston was outside and the door was firmly closed behind him, she dropped to the couch with a sigh.

I shook my head. I'd never seen a woman her age act so twitterpated. Especially not a married woman.

"I take it there's a history there?" I said, my voice teasing.

"We both grew up here. I've known him nearly my entire life. We tried to date a few times, but our timing was always off. One of us was leaving or dating or married."

"Is he married now?" I asked.

"His wife died a few months ago."

I didn't think it was my place to remind her that his wife may be dead, but her husband was still very much alive.

"I know what you're thinking," she said with a grin. "Don't you worry your pretty color-changing head. Clancy may not be handsome or friendly or—well—any of the things Weston is. But I'm not a cheating woman. If I was, Weston and I would have been together long ago."

"It's really not my business," I said. "But I'm happy to hear that."

She nodded once. "Now, let's get to work on that over-head bin work."

We started with empty suitcases—the specific ones she would take with her on the trip. Thankfully, she was relatively tall and would have no problem reaching the over-head bins. If she was short, it might have been more of a challenge.

The biggest problem we had was her range of motion. She didn't have much issue with strength, even when we loaded the suitcases. But once she got to right above her shoulder height, her arms didn't want to lift any higher.

She lowered a fully loaded carry-on suitcase to the floor and sighed. "This is more challenging than I thought it would be. I didn't realize my arms would give me such fits."

"If we keep working through it, we'll get your range of motion figured out," I said. "Or you could let Clancy help you."

She let out a burst of sarcastic laughter. "Clancy probably won't even go with me at this point."

"Couldn't convince him, huh?" I followed her into the kitchen, where she got us both glasses of water without ice.

"He's still angry I didn't fire you," she said, then took a sip of her water. Her face was red from the exertion.

A chime sounded, and we both glanced at the deck. It was the fifth time it had gone off since I'd been there. The first two times, we went to check it out. But every time we looked, there was no one there.

"Did you tell Clancy about that going off all the time?" I asked.

"He knows," she said. "He said we just have to stay vigilant, and it'll be okay. It's better to get fifty fake notifications if the fifty-first is real than to get zero and have someone break in."

"Does he think someone's really going to break in?"

"He's had threats." Renée shrugged. "But whether they're legitimate is debatable. I've heard rich people get this way." She downed the rest of her water and, before I could ask a follow-up question, was back at the luggage. "Let's get this figured out."

I finished my water and followed her.

Jasmine peeked into the room where we had been exercising. "I'm heading out. Do you need anything else before I go?"

"There's an envelope for you in the kitchen drawer," Renée said. "A bit of spending cash for your vacation."

Jasmine's eyes lit up. "Thank you so much."

When she was gone, Renée hoisted the heavy bag up and tried to get it above shoulder level.

"You need to take it slow," I said. "If you hurt yourself, you won't be able to tango."

She dropped the suitcase and smiled. "Are you serious?"

"Starting Saturday."

She threw her arms around my neck and squeezed with more strength than I thought she had in her. "This is the best day ever."

"Do you think you'll be able to get Clancy to come?" I asked when she released me.

"I can be very persuasive when I want to be." She quirked an eyebrow up at me, and we both laughed.

"I should probably go," I said. "Don't overdo the exercises while I'm gone. You could hurt yourself."

"I'll be okay," she said.

I gave her a mildly threatening look.

"I'm kidding."

"Good," I said. "Because we have to get you in tip-top shape so you can go to Argentina. With or without Clancy."

"Really?" an angry voice said behind me.

I whipped around to find Clancy glaring at me.

"I was kidding," I said, looking from Clancy to Renée and back again.

"Brainwashing." He pointed a finger and stepped toward me. "I bet you're the one who got her to hand the farm over to Weston, too. You're trying to edge me out of her life. And I won't have it."

My scalp was burning. This man meant business.

"She did nothing of the sort," Renée said, stepping between us, completely unafraid of her husband. "Weston and I go way back. It only seemed right to let him farm the land. He's willing to give us a great price."

"Oh, I'm sure he is," Clancy said, turning his anger on Renée. "I know all about your relationship with Weston, and he's not farming our land. I don't care how much he's willing to pay."

Renée crossed her arms over her chest. "It's triple what everyone else has offered."

Clancy seemed to lose his words.

"That's what I thought," Renée said, stepping away and pulling me toward the door by my arm. "Money talks, and Weston knows that."

"Well, I don't want him around you. I know his real motive for farming our property." Clancy's words were angrier and angrier.

"If I was going to run away with Weston," Renée said. "I would have done so by now. Your silly jealousy is completely unfounded."

Clancy looked like his head was going to explode.

"I'll see you Saturday," Renée said with a wink, opening the door and letting me out.

I didn't want to leave her alone with him. Not as mad as he was.

"Why don't you walk me out?" I asked.

Renée's face softened into a smile. "I'm okay. He gets this way sometimes." She lowered her voice. "He won't hurt me."

"What are you whispering to her?" Clancy yelled behind her.

"Clancy, that's enough," Renée said, then turned back to me. "I'll see you Saturday."

And with that, she closed the door, pushing me into the cold.

5

The rest of the week left me with an uneasy feeling. I wasn't sure if it was because of the way Renée and I had left things—even though she had texted me to tell me she was fine—or if it was because the mural was still without people.

Saturday afternoon, I climbed the hidden stairs behind the bookcase in my bedroom to see if my grandmother left any words of wisdom for me in her journal.

Penelope curled up at my feet as I gently opened the cover.

I had added my own words to the empty pages in the back—a way for me to document my struggles and achievements in life and with my magic. As I learned more and coaxed my magic from the dark place in the back of my mind, I jotted down the stories. Part of me felt like those words had been on the page all along, just waiting for me to write them.

Esme's part of the journal was in a language I couldn't decipher. By some sort of magic, the words translated themselves, revealing the messages to me when I needed them most. And today was no different.

I tried locating her today. My location skills have always worked, but somehow, I knew the magic wouldn't work for this. It's as if she's blocked me. As if she doesn't want me to find her.

I nearly dropped the journal. Esme had tried to find Emily. Using her magic. I didn't even know that was possible. I flipped through the pages, searching for another entry. One that might have talked about a successful attempt. But, of course, if it had been successful, Emily would be here now.

Right?

I closed the journal and returned it to the table next to the oversized chair I'd curled up in. Sometimes just being in the attic with the fairy lights shimmering all around me was enough to pick up my mood. But not today. Today's journal entry simply made me long for my mother even more than usual.

"Penelope, we should probably head down and get the barn ready for the dance class." I stood and stretched my arms over my head, then swan dived forward to stretch my back and legs. It had been too cold recently to get out under the moonlight for yoga, and my body was not as limber as it had been in Colorado. Needless to say, I couldn't wait for the warmer weather.

As we walked back down the staircase and closed the

bookshelf, I took in my surroundings. Sometimes it caught me off guard just how much my life had changed in a year.

A year ago, I'd been living in Mona with Penelope. That was just before I moved in with my last boyfriend. And just before he'd kicked me out after an argument.

Now, as I walked down the hallway toward the stairs leading to the main level, I felt my soul exhale. The farmhouse was larger than one person and a pig needed, but I'd had several guests in the short time I'd lived here. Each room had a name and would only welcome the person who was meant to stay there.

When I first moved in, I'd tried every room, unable to sleep for one reason or another. Finally, I gave in and slept in the master bedroom. And though I loved sleeping in the bed I used to make inside Mona, I'd never slept as well as I did now in Esme's bed.

I lifted Penelope into my arms before heading down the stairs. "How did we get so lucky?"

She snuggled into me as if she knew what I was talking about.

There wasn't much left to do in the barn. I'd already moved the equipment and set up the sound system. I'd created a playlist of beginner tango music on my phone and had brushed up on the steps.

As I was sweeping the floor, Xander walked in looking hotter than the sun in Florida. He wore all black—as usual —but his button-down shirt showed off his defined biceps, and his hair was pulled into a bun at the back of his head.

"What?" he asked, looking down at his shirt.

I averted my gaze. "Nothing, I just didn't expect you to get here so early."

He glanced at his phone. "I'm only five minutes early. Doesn't the class start at four?"

I swept the bits of dust and dirt into the dustpan and deposited them into the trash can. "I guess I lost track of the time."

"I wanted to come a bit early, so I knew what you expected of me," he said. "I've danced before, but I've never taught a class."

"Lucky for you, I've taught lots of classes."

He grinned, and my knees felt like they might give out. I needed to get myself together. If he and I were going to be dancing, I couldn't have him catching onto my nervousness . . . or my feelings.

"I figured we'd start with some of the steps without a partner," I said. "And then when they get those down, we can partner up and go from there."

"Do you think we need to give them a sample of what it'll look like?"

"Like a demonstration?" I asked, trying to keep my voice from shaking.

He shrugged.

"I, for one, would appreciate a demonstration," Amy said, walking through the door with Fran. She had an evil grin on her face.

"Me too," Katie said, coming in behind them. "Earl isn't sure this is quite his thing. I think you two need to show us."

She nudged Earl in the ribs.

"Uh, yeah," he said. "Demonstrate."

I laughed and snuck a peek at Xander, who looked like he might have actually been blushing a bit. Or maybe I was just projecting my feelings onto him.

"Let's wait until the others get here," I said. "And then we can do a quick demonstration before we start the lesson."

Amy and Katie looked pleased with themselves.

Hank and Nancy came in next. Of all the couples, they were the most dressed up. Katie looked fabulous, as always, in her black leggings and black and white swirled shift dress. Amy and Fran looked like they did most days —Amy in her punk rock t-shirt and Fran in her jeans and flannel. But Hank and Nancy wore matching red outfits. Nancy wore a red dress with sparkles on the skirt, and Hank wore a matching sparkly red button-down with pressed black pants.

Everyone let out oohs and ahhs as Hank spun Nancy, causing her dress to twirl out a bit.

"We've been dancing for years," Hank said. "But we've never learned to tango."

The fact that he looked excited to dance with his wife warmed my heart. They were like tattooed dancing Santa and Mrs. Claus.

"Who else is coming?" Nancy asked.

"I put up some fliers in the café and the library," I said. "And Renée said she and Clancy would be here."

"Am I in the right place?" Weston asked, peeking his head in the door.

I caught Nancy and Katie exchange a glance.

"Are you here for the tango classes?" I asked. Thankfully, I'd kept the surprise out of my voice. I didn't think

Renée would have invited him to the class, but I could have been wrong.

"Yep," he said. "I saw a flyer for it at the café."

"Then you're in the right place," I said.

"Looks like I'm the odd one out," he said, glancing around at the couples.

"There's still time," Katie said. "Another single lady might have seen the sign."

As if on cue, Bonnie came walking through the door.

Katie, Amy, and Nancy looked so delighted by this, I thought they might faint.

"Tango classes, right?" Bonnie asked as we all stared at her.

"Right," I said. "Come on in."

Katie grabbed Weston by the arm and dragged him toward Bonnie. "Bonnie, this is Weston. His wife recently died."

Bonnie held out a hand. "Nice to meet you."

Weston smiled politely but looked over her shoulder at the door as if waiting for someone else to walk in. Someone married, perhaps? I held in my groan.

"Bonnie's—uh—partner, just died too," Katie said, trying to bring Weston's attention back to the beautiful, *single* woman standing in front of him.

"I'm so sorry for your loss," Weston said as if automatically.

"Thank you," Bonnie said, taking her hand back and giving me a questioning glance.

I shook my head in an attempt to get across that I had not set this up to play matchmaker.

"It's four," Xander said, coming to stand beside me.

I glanced at the door. Renée had sworn she was coming. But maybe Clancy had talked her out of it. "We'll wait five more minutes to see if there are any stragglers, and then we'll start."

"With a demonstration," Katie said.

I smiled as my scalp tingled. Penelope oinked, and everyone laughed.

Everyone but Weston, who gaped at my changing hair.

"It's all right," Fran said, patting him on the back a little too hard. "She won't hurt you."

Almost everyone in town was used to my hair changing since they knew Esme and Emily, who both had the same magic.

"You remember Esme, don't you?" Katie asked. "You were probably a few years ahead of her in school, but she lived in this house."

"My family stayed away from the Vanderwicks," he said, his tone apologetic. "I didn't know why until now."

"That's ridiculous," Fran said. "The Vanderwicks never hurt anyone."

He nodded. "My parents were fearful of many things—things they didn't understand. Thankfully, I did not inherit that gene."

Fran looked accepting of his answer, and we all settled into a bit of small talk about the weather and the cold that was irking everyone.

Five minutes passed and then ten, and the only people to show up were Bex and Laura. Bex wore colorful geometric leggings and a black sweater. Laura, who looked like she'd gotten her arm twisted into coming, wore a simple gray dress.

"I suppose we should get started," I said.

I'd have to call Renée after class if she didn't show up. But right now, I had a barn full of paying customers and, even though they were my friends, I still needed to be professional.

I pressed play on my phone, and music filled the air.

"You ready?" I asked Xander.

He smiled and wrapped his arm around me, sending zaps of electricity throughout my body. "Ready as I'll ever be."

6

The way Xander held me—tight but gentle—made dancing with him a joy like I'd never felt. He led but gave me room for my own self-expression.

We started slowly, testing each other's abilities.

I tried to ignore the feel of his hand moving from my spine to my side and back as we glided across the floor.

The music filled my ears as I watched Xander's eyes. He had an intensity about him that was more pronounced when he danced.

As the music increased in pace, our steps did as well. Though we'd never practiced before, it was as if we were one. As if he could read my mind, and I could read his.

He held me firm as I lowered into a split and pulled me up into a complicated twisting lift.

I felt weightless. I'd never had such a capable partner.

When he lowered me back to my feet, his nose nearly touching mine, I knew the music was ending.

But I didn't want it to.

I could have danced with him for hours. No part of me felt exerted. Instead, my body was alive.

The music stopped, but he and I stayed in the hold. His lips dangerously close to mine.

He could have kissed me. I wouldn't have objected. I still dreamed of the kiss we shared a few weeks before.

When the applause broke out, I felt the bubble burst.

I'd almost—no—I'd completely forgotten we were demonstrating. For an entire group of people.

All of whom were now staring at us.

Xander and I separated faster than two teenagers caught under the bleachers during a football game.

"I don't know about the rest of you, but I don't think my back will take that sort of dancing," Hank said, his rosy cheeks balled up with his smile.

I cleared my throat. "We were just demonstrating what the tango *could* look like. Obviously, we'll be teaching you a much easier version."

"That's good because that lifty-spinny thing you did made my back hurt just watching," Fran said.

I let out a nervous laugh, still trying to get my bearings back. "Okay, then," I said. "Let's begin."

By the time the class had ended, everyone had a decent grasp on the basic steps, and a few people even stayed a bit longer to perfect their steps.

Bonnie and Weston had partnered together, but he'd spent most of the time staring at the door. I had a feeling the two of them wouldn't be going out together any time soon. Especially when he bolted the minute class was over. I'd be surprised if he even came back for another class at all.

"That seemed to go well," Xander said when everyone had headed out.

"I think so too." I tried not to think about our dance. Other than during the initial demonstration, we hadn't touched. The basic steps didn't require touching, anyway. "Here's half of what I made." I handed him a check.

"I never asked you to pay me," he said, not taking it.

"But you're instructing just as much as I am."

He laughed. "I just stand in the back and nod along with you. I'd hardly call that instructing."

I dropped my hand. "Then can I at least buy you dinner?"

"Deal," he said. "But only if it comes with a movie."

"I'll get changed."

"Why? You look great."

I glanced down at my red skirt and tight black shirt. "I should probably put on some boots at least." And do something better with my hair. There were no movie theaters in Cliff Haven, so we'd have to travel into the city. And in the city, people didn't know about my hair.

We went inside, Penelope trotting along with us.

I pulled on my boots and tied my hair up into a scarf.

"You don't have to hide it," Xander said.

"Easy for you to say." I glanced at his hair. "Your magic isn't on display for everyone to see."

"Your magic is beautiful," he said, reaching up and untying the scarf. My hair fell around my shoulders in loose pink waves. "Anyone who is afraid of it will have to deal with me."

Sometimes I hated it when he tried to protect me, but right now, it felt nice. Comforting.

Penelope let out a low oink.

Xander took a step back. "Sorry." He cleared his throat. "I'll go warm up the truck."

"It's not a big deal," I said, following him out the door. "I still have a magic jacket to keep me warm."

He glanced back at me and smiled. "I never did get that back from you, did I?"

"I suppose I wanted to keep it."

"Consider it yours," he said as he opened the passenger door for me. In the summer, he rode a motorcycle, but in the winter, he drove a massive black pickup truck. Thankfully, I was wearing leggings under my skirt, as there was no graceful way to hoist myself into the passenger seat.

He gently closed my door, and I smiled. We'd hung out before, but this felt like an actual date.

I didn't want to get my hopes up, but he *had* called my magic beautiful.

Penelope stood in front of the truck as we backed out. I waved, but she didn't seem to be looking at me. She seemed to be staring—or rather, glaring—at Xander.

He let out a nervous laugh. "That's some pig you have."

"She's definitely something." She'd never tried to warn me away from a man. Even the ones who ended up breaking my heart. I pushed the thought away. She was just a pig.

Xander hummed along to the radio as we made our way down the dusty gravel roads toward the main highway.

"Have you heard from Harriet?" Xander asked when the song concluded.

"No," I said. "Not yet."

Harriet was a cousin I hadn't known I had until a few weeks ago. She'd come to town as quickly as she left, leaving me with more questions than answers. She thought someone was going to give her information about how her mother had died. Then someone else died, and Harriet thought she had been the actual target of the murder. When she didn't get any closer to finding her mother's killer, she vanished.

Thinking about it brought tears to my eyes.

"I'm sorry," Xander said. "I didn't mean to upset you."

"It's okay. I'm okay. I just wish I'd found out something about my mother." I looked out the window. "At least I got a picture of her."

The picture was taken in the hospital after she had me. It was probably one of the last times she'd seen me—before she left me at a fire station and disappeared.

As we drove, a thought popped into my head. "Do you mind if we check on something before we head into the city?"

"Sure." Xander stopped and waited for me to give him directions.

"I don't think you've met her, but Renée told me she would be at the dance classes."

"And she never showed up."

"Yeah," I said. "Can we drive past her house really quick? I don't think it's too late to stop by."

"Do you think you should call first?"

Something told me I needed to physically go to her house. A feeling. Part of my magic.

But calling did seem like the right thing to do. Especially if Clancy was there, which he probably was.

I pulled out my phone as Xander patiently waited at the stop sign. There was hardly any traffic, especially on the gravel road.

I dialed her number. It rang a few times, then her voice came on and asked me to leave a message.

"Hey, Renée," I said after the beep. "I noticed you weren't in dance class tonight, and I wanted to make sure you were okay. I'm going to stop by your house here in a minute. If you get this before I get there, call me back. Thanks."

I hung up.

"Where to?" Xander asked.

"Take a right."

He turned the truck in the direction opposite the way we would have gone to the city.

"Do you think something's wrong?" Xander asked.

"I'm not sure," I said. "Maybe. It's strange she didn't come to class. She and Clancy had a big fight the last time I was there. She texted me afterward and told me she was okay, but I still worry."

"Who is Clancy?"

"Her husband. He's a mean guy." I pointed up ahead. "Turn left where that white car just pulled out."

He slowed and turned down another gravel road. "Do you think he'd hurt her?"

"She didn't seem to think so," I said. "But I wouldn't put it past him. He was not happy about her and Weston."

"As in the Weston who was at dance classes tonight?"

"They dated a while back, and apparently, the flame still burns there," I said. "I wouldn't be surprised if he had only come to steal a dance."

"That's why he didn't even look at Bonnie."

"And why he probably won't be back if Renée's not going to come."

We passed a couple of houses and then came to Renée's.

"This is it," I said, and Xander pulled into the driveway.

Clancy's fancy car was in the driveway, along with a pickup I didn't recognize.

"The door is wide open," Xander said. "We need to be careful."

Adrenaline pulsed through my chest, up my neck, and into my scalp. Something was wrong. No one in their right mind left the door open with the temperature outside.

The minute Xander's truck came to a stop, I opened the door and ran toward the house. Before I could make it, I slipped and fell against the hood of the truck. It was still warm.

Whoever it belonged to had just gotten there.

Xander helped me up and followed me toward the front door.

The house was dark inside, but I'd been there enough to know where I was going.

I tiptoed toward the kitchen. If someone was inside, they might be dangerous. The last thing I wanted to do was alert them to my presence.

Not that I felt particularly unsafe. My magic wasn't powerful enough to protect me in any meaningful way, but Xander's was. At least, I thought it was.

The kitchen was as dark as the rest of the house, but with the windows and the moon shining in, it was easy to see the figure holding a knife.

7

I froze.

Xander was standing right behind me. I'd only seen him use his magic a few times, but I wasn't worried in the slightest that a man with a knife could overpower him.

What I was worried about was what we'd see when we turned on the lights.

"Drop the knife." Xander's deep voice rumbled behind me.

The figure seemed to turn toward us. "I didn't do anything. Someone else was here—he went out that door."

"Put the knife on the ground and walk away," Xander said.

I reached for the light switch on the wall. Whatever we were facing would be easier in the light. Even if I didn't want to face it.

"I was just checking—" The man's words cut off as he seemed to slip and fall out of sight.

I flipped on the lights and held my breath.

The man rolled onto his side, and I gasped.

Weston's shirt, along with the floor, the appliances, and several cupboards, were stained with blood.

"Don't move," Xander said. "Ellie, call Jake."

My brain was still trying to process what I was seeing.

There was a body underneath Weston.

"Ellie." Xander's voice sounded like it was coming from the end of a long tunnel.

The body.

I couldn't see the face, but the rest of it definitely wasn't Renée.

This realization seemed to break the trance I was in. Well, that and Xander's nudge to my shoulder.

"Call. Jake."

"I didn't do this," Weston said, still holding the knife. "I wanted to check on Renée, and this is what I found. The man—the one who did it—he ran out the sliding door."

I pulled out my phone and dialed Jake's number.

Weston was still on the ground next to the body. Still covered in blood. I sucked in a breath and averted my eyes so I wouldn't be sick.

The rest of the house was a disaster. It was amazing Xander and I hadn't tripped on anything walking in through the dark.

"Hello?" Jake said.

"Hey," I said. "I'm at the Wright's, and there's a body."

I could hear the scrape of a chair in the background. "I'm not in town," Jake said. "But I'll be there as soon as I can."

"Oh, and there's a man—Weston Peters—with a knife, covered in blood. He's alive."

Jake's voice deepened. "Are you in danger?"

"No," I said. "I don't think so." My hair hadn't indicated any sort of danger. "Xander has him covered."

"Good," Jake said. "I'll call Deb."

"Thanks."

He disconnected the phone call.

"The police are on their way," I said.

"I swear," Weston said, trying to stand. "I didn't do this. I found him like this."

"Don't move," Xander said. "Trust me. You don't want to take me on in a fight."

"I don't want to fight anyone," Weston said.

"When did you get here?" I asked.

"Just before you," he said. "I wouldn't have had enough time to make this kind of mess."

"Why were you walking around in the dark?" Xander asked.

"When I came in, I flipped on the lights and saw Clancy lying there." He rolled further away from the body, and I realized the body was Clancy. "I turned the lights back off because I didn't know if whoever did this was still inside. And sure enough, the minute I turned them off, a guy bolted through that door."

"How'd you get all bloody?" I asked.

Weston looked down at himself. "Oh. Oh my." That was all he said before he turned and vomited all over Clancy's body.

"Now, you've ruined the crime scene," Xander said. "Don't do that."

Weston was still heaving.

"Close your eyes," I said.

Weston did.

"Think of somewhere you'd like to be right now," I said. "Anywhere but here."

"Argentina," he mumbled.

I sighed. It didn't look good for him. If he broke in and killed Clancy, he might have done it to have Renée all to himself.

Xander took the knife out of Weston's hand, checked Clancy for a pulse, and then helped Weston to his feet.

"Did you see Renée here?" I asked, glancing around.

"I didn't get very far, but no," Weston said.

"Are you certain whoever was in the house left?" I asked.

"Pretty certain," Weston said.

"I'm going to go see if I can find Renée," I told Xander.

Xander looked torn but probably knew he wouldn't be able to talk me out of it. "Be careful."

As I was making my way toward the stairs, the lights of a police car came blazing through the front windows.

Deb and another officer walked through the door, guns drawn.

"Is there anyone else in the house?" Deb asked me.

"I don't think so," I said. "I was just about to go upstairs and try to find Renée—the owner of the house. I'm worried she might be in trouble."

"You wait here," Deb said. "I'll check it out."

"Renée is my friend." I followed her up the steps. "Don't worry. I'll stay out of the way."

Deb was Bex's older sister and had come to tolerate me since I'd helped on other cases.

"If I let you get hurt, Jake will never forgive me," she said but didn't prevent me from following her up the stairs.

"Where is Jake, anyway?" I asked. "Don't you usually work together?"

"He took the night off."

I waited for her to say more, but she didn't.

The entire upper level was clear besides every room being ransacked.

"It looks like whoever did this was looking for something," I said.

"What makes you think the man we apprehended didn't do this?" Deb asked.

"A feeling, I guess," I said.

Deb was all too aware of my feelings. Esme—my grandmother—used to have them too and had often helped Jake with cases. But feelings weren't evidence. They weren't admissible in court.

"Let's try downstairs," Deb said.

Whoever had come into the house had to have been there for a good amount of time to do all the damage. That, or there had been multiple people.

Deb and I checked in each room, but Renée was nowhere to be found.

"Anything?" Xander asked as we made our way back to the kitchen.

"Just a big mess," I said. "Maybe there's a basement?"

Deb shook her head. "Only a crawlspace. We'll check it

out, but with the weather as cold as it's been and the outdoor access, I'd guess it's frozen and covered in snow."

"Then where is Renée?"

"We'll talk to Weston," Deb said. "Maybe he did something with her."

I shook my head. "There's no way he hurt her. He loved her."

"Maybe she denied his advances, and he lashed out in a rage," Deb said. "We have to keep an open mind. He was covered in blood, holding a knife that was also covered in blood."

"He threw up at the sight of the blood," I said.

"He threw up all over the body," Deb said. "Maybe he was trying to ruin the evidence."

"Or maybe the sight of blood makes him sick," I said.

She shrugged. "We'll talk to him."

I didn't like that she was dismissing me, but I wasn't a police officer. Technically, I had nothing to do with this investigation.

Other than the fact that one of my friends was missing and her house was completely messed up.

"When you got here, what did you see?" Deb asked, pulling out a notebook and pen. A team of officers walked around the room, placing little markers where they thought evidence might be.

"The door was open," I said. "The front door. Weston's truck was in the driveway. I slipped and fell against the hood. The engine was still warm." I glanced at Xander. "That would mean he'd only just gotten here like he said."

"Keep going," Deb said. "What did you see when you walked inside?"

I pushed down my frustration and her brushing off my comment. "It was dark, but with the moonlight shining through the windows, we could see a man's figure holding a knife."

"Was he covered in blood at that point?" Deb asked.

"It was too dark to tell," I said. "And he fell on top of Clancy's body before I got to the lights."

"So it's possible that the blood on his shirt came from falling in the blood on the floor," Xander said.

Deb didn't respond. "Anything else?"

"I called Jake, and we waited for you to get here."

"Did Weston say anything?"

"He kept saying he didn't do it and that someone else was in the house and left out that door," I said, pointing to the sliding glass door. "And then he threw up."

"And wanted to go to Argentina," Xander said with a laugh.

Deb's gaze darted up. "Why did he say he wanted to go to Argentina?"

"I told him to close his eyes and think of somewhere he'd like to be," I said. "I was trying to get his mind off the blood so he wouldn't throw up again."

"Wasn't Renée planning a trip to Argentina?" Deb asked.

Small towns were notorious for gossip, and Cliff Haven was no exception.

"She *and Clancy* were planning a trip to Argentina," I said. "I highly doubt they would have taken Weston with them."

"Unless Clancy was dead," Xander said, and I had the sudden urge to stomp on his foot.

Deb nodded and kept taking notes. "Anything else?"

"No," I said. "But for what it's worth, I stand by the opinion that Weston didn't do this."

Xander looked over at me, his eyes skeptical, but he said nothing.

"I'll keep that in mind," Deb said with a smirk. "I'm sure you have better things to do tonight than hang out at a crime scene."

My mind rushed back to the date Xander and I had planned. I'd been so excited, but now all I wanted to do was find Renée and make sure she was okay.

I glanced up at the room one more time. "Don't forget to put one there," I said to the officer with the markers.

"Where?" she asked.

"The sliding door," I said. "There's blood on the handle, and it's partially open."

She glanced over at it. "Thanks."

I turned and started toward the front door, Xander following behind me.

The door opened before we got there, and Jake walked in looking like he'd just stepped out of a men's formal-wear catalog. He had on a dark blue pinstripe suit with shiny shoes and little star cufflinks.

"Wow," I said. "You look nice."

He blushed. "I was at a show."

"I didn't know you liked—" My voice caught in my throat when a woman walked in behind him wearing an evening gown.

8

J ake noticed the look on my face and turned to see the woman he was apparently at a show with standing behind him. She was tall and blonde and drop-dead gorgeous.

"Oh, yes," he said. "Ellie, this is Georgia. My—"

"Girlfriend," Georgia said. "It's nice to finally meet you. Jake's told me so much about you."

Funny. He never mentioned her. I glanced at him, but he was looking past me at the crime scene.

"Uh, we were just leaving," Xander said.

"Right," Jake said. "Deb got all the information?"

I nodded, unable to form words.

"Good," he said. "If we need anything else, we'll call you."

Georgia smiled sweetly as we walked through the door and into the cold.

Xander opened the door of his pickup for me, and I climbed inside.

"What do you want to do?" Xander asked after he started the truck and blasted the heat.

"There's nothing much we can do," I said. "She seems nice enough. And pretty. And if he wants to date, he should be able to date."

"I meant about dinner and the movie," Xander said, his smile sweet and slightly teasing.

"Oh, right," I said. Why it bothered me so much that Jake was dating was beyond me. He wasn't my father—we'd established that almost immediately after I'd moved to Cliff Haven. And we didn't know whether my mother was even still alive. She'd left town and never spoke to him again. That was over twenty years ago. He shouldn't have to wait around for her to return. She might never return.

A lump formed in my throat at the thought of never meeting my mother. Never being able to ask her all the questions I had. But that was a distinct possibility. One I'd grappled with my entire life.

"I think I should just go home tonight," I said. "The whole crime scene thing made me lose my appetite, and I'm exhausted."

"Understandable." He put the truck in reverse and slowly made his way back to my house.

When he pulled into my driveway, I turned and said, "I still owe you dinner and a movie. I won't forget."

"I won't either," he said, reaching over and grabbing my hand, sending a hum of electricity up my arm. "And El?"

I looked up into his gorgeous green eyes. "Yeah?"

"Don't worry about Jake. I'm sure he knows what he's getting into with her."

He thought I was worried about her breaking Jake's heart. "Thanks," I said, unable to tell him the truth. Especially since I couldn't really figure out the truth for myself. It was completely unreasonable to be upset with him for moving on with his life after twenty-some years. Even if he was moving on from my mother.

"I'll see you tomorrow for dance class?" I asked.

"I wouldn't miss it for the world."

I closed his truck door and walked to the house. Penelope was on her side, dreaming, when I walked through the front door. I tip-toed to the kitchen so I wouldn't frighten her and opened the refrigerator door.

But I wasn't hungry. Not because of the crime scene, but because of the uneasiness I felt about Jake having a girlfriend. A girlfriend who knew about me. Which meant they had to have been together for a while.

No.

I shook my head.

I would not let this get to me.

It was stupid.

I was acting as if he was my father and had just introduced me to my evil stepmother.

I closed the refrigerator door, probably harder than was necessary, turned with my back to it, and slid to the floor, holding my knees to my chest.

The slamming of the refrigerator door must have alarmed Penelope because her squeals came from the front hall.

"It's just me," I said, but either she didn't hear me or

was on a mission because she charged through her piggy door to go take care of the mysterious noise that had awoken her slumber.

I chuckled. At least Penelope could still make me laugh.

Pushing to my feet, I exhaled the thoughts about Jake's love life out of my brain.

Besides, Jake was the last of my worries right now. Renée was still missing and could be hurt . . . or a suspect.

I really didn't want to consider the second option, but I couldn't help it. The more I thought about the facts, the more it seemed like Weston hadn't killed Clancy.

Meaning someone else had.

I needed to find Renée, and fast.

But how?

Something in the back of my mind clicked. Esme had used her magic to try to find Emily. What if I could use mine to find Renée?

It seemed pretty far-fetched, but I had to try.

My magic was by no means mature, but I'd used it both successfully and unsuccessfully in the past. What could it hurt to try to locate Renée? It wasn't like I was trying to bring someone back from the dead or something.

I stood over the island countertop in the kitchen and focused on the voice in my head. What was it telling me? What was my hair feeling?

My gaze darted around, trying to find the specks of magic that sometimes hung in the air. The edges of magic, Harriet had once called it.

I focused.

Renée.

She was out there. I could sense that.

My hair follicles tingled.

Is she dead?

I pondered the question, turning it over in my mind.

No.

She wasn't dead.

Is she hurt?

I thought harder.

Is she hurt?

Nothing.

I moved on.

Where is she?

I needed a location.

I pictured her house. The fireplace and the kitchen. The garage. The driveway.

She'd driven somewhere.

I didn't get a chance to look in the garage, but if I had to bet, I'd say her car wasn't there.

The thoughts running through my head stopped abruptly.

I needed to go to her garage.

But Jake was there. With his girlfriend.

I'd just have to put on my big girl underpants and deal with it. I visualized the silliest set of underpants, acted like I was putting them on, then put my hands on my hips and squared my shoulders.

I could do this.

With a nod, I started toward the door.

But sitting behind me was a confused-looking Penelope with her piggy ears up and folded over, her head cocked to the side.

"Did you get whoever made that loud noise?" I laughed.

She still stared at me with a questioning expression.

"What is it?" I knelt to the ground and patted my legs. "Come here."

She stood slowly from her seated position, her nose wiggling, taking in my scent.

"Why are you acting so strange?"

An oink I'd never heard from her rumbled in her throat. It wasn't a warning oink or an excited oink or even a mad oink. It was more of a questioning oink.

When I glimpsed my hair out of the corner of my eye, I understood immediately.

My hair was a shimmery pastel-colored rainbow.

It was also longer than it ever had been, pooling around my feet as I crouched on the ground.

"Okay, that's strange," I said, lifting a strand off the floor. "Maybe it's because I used my magic?"

Penelope took a couple of steps toward me but was still outside my grasp. I wouldn't force her to come to me. If she didn't feel comfortable, who was I to tell her she was wrong?

What did I know? Maybe I looked weird in other ways. Or maybe my magic could be dangerous to her. I'd never forgive myself if somehow I hurt her with my magic.

I stood and marched down the hall to find the small mirror hanging next to some old photographs of Esme. My face looked the same as usual, but my hair was definitely different.

"I don't have time to worry about this right now," I

said. "I have to go see if I can find another clue to where Renée might be."

I wrapped my hair in a ballerina bun, securing it with a large scrunchie from the basket by the front door. "I'll see you later."

Penelope just watched as I grabbed my jacket and headed out the door.

9

T he police were still at Renée and Clancy's when I got there, but thankfully, Jake's pickup was gone. Not that I was allowing myself to care.

I walked up to the door and let myself in.

"Hey, back so soon?" The officer I showed the bloody door handle asked. I didn't see Deb, which would probably make my life even easier.

"Yeah," I said. "I realized I forgot my purse in the back of Renée's car from the last time we did seatbelt exercises. I didn't know if I'd be able to get it? Now that my mind is on it, I won't be able to sleep."

"Seatbelt exercises?" She looked at me like I was crazy.

"Oh, yeah," I said, thankful that was the part of the story she latched onto. "When people get older, they can lose certain functions, so I work with them on their range of motion and strength so they can be independent in their daily lives. Renée—Clancy's wife—wanted to go to Argentina, but to do that, she would have to fly. We were working on buckling her seatbelt, lifting her luggage into the overhead compartment, and getting it off the baggage claim carousel."

Most people hadn't ever heard of what I did, but once I explained it, they understood. "That sounds really cool," she said. "My grandma lives in the assisted living home in town. She has such a hard time tying her shoes that we just bought her slip-ons. But I remember how sad she seemed that day."

"I'd be happy to help her," I said. "Maybe I can get her back into laced shoes."

The officer's eyes lit up. "Do you think that's possible?"

"I'd have to do an evaluation, but I've seen lots of progress with my techniques." And my magic. But I wasn't about to tell her that.

"I could pay you, of course," the officer said. "But that would be fantastic."

I handed her one of the business cards I kept in the back of my phone case. "Call me sometime, and I can put her on the schedule."

She slipped it into her shirt pocket. "Thank you so much."

"And about getting my purse? Is the garage part of the crime scene or . . ?"

"Nope," she said. "Go right ahead. Just close the door on the way out."

She turned to walk back to the crime scene but stopped when I asked, "Did you find any other clues?"

When she glanced back at me, she smiled and crossed her arms over her chest. "Jake told me you liked to help with cases."

I shrugged. "I guess it runs in the family."

"I loved Esme," she said. "She was the sweetest woman. And sharp as a tack. It's too bad she died."

I nodded.

"But yes, we did find some additional clues," she said. "Come look."

I desperately wanted to get to the garage to find Renée, but I was also curious.

"We haven't confirmed this since we're not the coroner," she whispered, glancing around. The other officers were busy and out of earshot. "It doesn't look like he was stabbed, but maybe once here." She pointed to Clancy's shoulder. There was a rip in the fabric and what looked like a knife puncture, but there wasn't any blood coming from the wound.

"Then where did all this blood come from?" I motioned to the surrounding floor.

"It probably looks like more than it really is," she said. "But I'd guess it came from the back of his head, where his skull took quite the beating. Do you want to see?"

I shook my head. "I'll take your word for it."

She shrugged as if seeing someone's bashed-in head wasn't a big deal at all. "We also found a handprint on the deck out here."

She led me out the door, careful to use her gloved hand to open the door.

The bloody handprint was closer to the stairs than the door.

"Do you think someone tripped?" I asked. "Maybe whoever did this?"

"I'd say it's a possibility," she said. "And if that's the

case, then maybe they escaped on foot. We'll look for foot-prints tomorrow in the daylight." She checked her watch. "Which isn't too far off."

As we walked back inside, a chime went off, alerting us to our own presence.

"Oh," I said. "That's the security system. Maybe there's some sort of data to be taken from it."

"We haven't been able to find the main control panel," she said. "Did Renée ever tell you about it?"

"Only that it was on her phone," I said. "I bet it's on Clancy's, too, if you check."

"We definitely will when we find his phone," she said. "Thanks. And I'll call you about my grandma."

We said goodbye, and I headed toward the garage. If it hadn't been for adrenaline, I probably would have fallen asleep standing up. I yawned. I had an early shift at the café in only a few hours, but I'd operated on less sleep in my life. Now was not the time for sleep.

I flipped on the garage light to find what I expected—Renée's car was missing.

Other cars took up space further down, but the spot where Renée's car was always parked was empty. I took a step into the garage and then tried to focus on my magic.

My hair felt heavy on my head. If it grew every time I used my magic, I would have to form stronger neck muscles.

Where did she go?

I closed my eyes and imagined the words floating through my mind, leading me to her location. At first, it was dark as if I had on a blindfold. Maybe someone had taken Renée and blindfolded her.

But then lights blazed on so bright my eyes watered beneath my eyelids. I pushed my magic harder. The light dimmed slowly. I could feel my hair changing again, but it definitely wasn't getting heavier.

In my head, the images were blurry. I couldn't make out where I was—where she was.

But when a sound I knew all too well pierced through my vision, I knew all too well where she was.

Penelope's oink sent shivers down my neck.

Something was wrong.

My eyes flew open, and I half-expected to see Penelope standing in front of me. But the only thing in front of me was an empty garage. I took one last glance around and almost turned the light back off, but something stopped me.

A piece of paper was on the ground.

I didn't pick it up since I wasn't wearing gloves, but I didn't need to pick it up to read it.

Give me what I need, or else.

The words were typed on what looked like heavy recycled paper. There was no letterhead or signature. Just the single line.

My thoughts were all over the place.

Penelope was in trouble.

Or maybe Renée was.

Maybe someone kidnapped her.

Or she found the note and ran.

I rushed into the house and found the officer I'd been speaking to before.

"I need to show you something in the garage," I said.

Her face twisted from a smile to serious as she followed me back out.

I pointed to the note, and she crouched down to read it. "Or else."

She seemed to contemplate the implications, but I didn't have time to sit and stew about it with her. "I have to get home," I said. "But if you need anything else from me, let me know."

Thankfully, she was too distracted by the note to stop me.

I was back in Mona and tearing down the gravel road within seconds.

The roads were snow-covered, and Mona didn't have the best winter tires, but I pushed her nonetheless. We'd driven through worse together. "We need to get to Penelope," I said. "Just stay on the road."

Her metal steering wheel warmed beneath my touch, and I knew there was no way we'd get in an accident.

The house looked normal when I pulled up. All the lights were off like I'd left them. I pulled Mona into the garage and went out the big garage door. I'd close it after I got everything settled. If my hunch was right, Renée was somewhere on my property—probably with Penelope.

The door opened easily, and I called, "Penelope, where are you?"

I stopped to listen but heard nothing but my own breathing.

Through the house and out the back door, I ran toward the barn. Penelope couldn't get in there herself—there was no piggy door to the studio—but if someone else was in there, they could have easily missed her sneaking in.

I peeked through the door to find the lights on and music playing.

But there was no one in plain sight.

"Penelope?" I whispered. "Are you in here?"

A muffled oink, a scream, and then a squeal came from behind the sheet I had draped across the back of the barn. Where the mural was.

If someone messed with my pig or my mural, I couldn't be sure what my emotions would do with my magic. I sucked in a breath and said, "Give me my pig and get out of my barn."

"You don't have to do this," Renée's voice said. "I know nothing."

"Do what?" I asked. "Renée? Is that you? It's me, Ellie. Please, just let Penelope go. She has nothing to do with this."

"How do I know you weren't in on it?" she asked. "How can I be sure?"

I took a quiet step toward the back of the barn. "In on what?"

"Like I know," she said. "Maybe Clancy was right. Maybe you were just after my money. Leaving threatening notes to scare me."

"How many notes did you get?"

"Why? Are you trying to make sure I got them all? Because I did. And I destroyed them. Every last one."

"Except the one in the garage. Not that I wrote them," I added quickly. "I was looking for your car. I thought you might have left the house. There was a note on heavy recycled paper in the garage."

"So maybe I missed one," she said. "I guess you would know where they all were."

"Renée," I said. "You're my friend. I wouldn't do anything to hurt you or try to steal your money. In fact, I can refund you for all of your lessons if that would be helpful. Just please don't hurt Penelope."

At the sound of her name, Penelope let out an oink that sounded like a cry.

Tears welled in my eyes. If she did anything to hurt Penelope, I didn't know what I'd do.

Never knowing my mother and grandmother was hard. My cousin leaving without so much as a goodbye wasn't exactly pleasant. But Penelope had been with me for years. She was my best friend. A life without her might break me.

"If you think I did something wrong," I said. "Hurt me. Get me."

"You'll just use your magic on me."

Tears streaked down my cheeks. "Why did you come here?"

"I wasn't going to." I heard footsteps behind the curtain as if she was moving closer to me. "But after a few days, I realized I couldn't run forever. I had to meet you head-on. I could never be free unless I could live without fear."

"And I'm happy to help you live without fear," I said. "I didn't write those letters. I don't want your money. But I can help you find who did write them. I promise. I'll find them and they'll go to jail and they won't hurt you."

The curtain moved, and Renée peeked out from behind it. "You swear on your pig's life you didn't do it?"

I nodded so vigorously the scrunchie on top of my head fell to the floor, letting my hair flow to the ground. It wasn't a pastel color anymore. It was a deep red, edging on black. And the sparkles were gone.

I pushed it out of the way over my shoulders and felt it brushing against my calves through my leggings.

"I swear I didn't do it," I said. "I wouldn't threaten you."

She took a step out and let Penelope to the ground.

Penelope ran as fast as I'd ever seen, straight into my outstretched arms. My hair twisted into curls and turned a shade of deep purple. "Thank you for not hurting her."

Renée stepped out from behind the curtain, looking like she'd just gotten in a fistfight with a bear. Her hair was all ratted, her clothes torn, and what looked like blood covered her shins and forearms.

"I think you should come inside. I'll make you some hot cocoa—definitely not as good as yours, but good enough—and you can take a shower."

"Then what?"

"Then we can have a chat so we can figure out who is sending you these letters."

She looked like a frightened animal.

"Come on," I said, taking slow steps toward her before

slipping a cautious arm around her shoulder. "I probably even have some clothes you can borrow."

She wrapped her jacket tighter around her, though with all the tears in the fabric, I wasn't sure how well it would work.

I tried not to focus on the blood-like substance caked on her arms. If it was blood, she'd instantly become a suspect in Clancy's murder. What if she and Weston had worked together?

I shivered at the thought that my arm was wrapped around a potential murderer.

The house was still dark when we went inside. Penelope walked through her door before I opened the big door.

When I flipped on the lights, Renée raised her arms to cover her eyes.

"What happened to your wrists?" I asked when I saw the large gashes on her wrists.

"Nothing." She dropped them. "Where's the shower?"

I walked her up the stairs to the long hallway leading to several rooms. "Why don't you choose the room that feels right, and I'll get you some fresh towels?"

She looked at me suspiciously but started down the hallway anyway.

I grabbed a couple of towels and washrags from the linen closet at the end of the hall. The first door Renée tried was to Rainbow, but the knob didn't turn in her grip. That was probably for the best. Rainbow was a rather cheery room with its bright pink walls and purple ceiling. Not exactly the mood Renée seemed to be in right now.

Luna and Dewdrop both seemed to be locked as well.

"Okay, do you want to just give me the key to one?" Renée asked, reaching the door to Firefly.

"The right one will open," I said. "Trust me." I was still learning the magical properties of the house, but the bedrooms were slightly less of a mystery than the rest. They only allowed the person they wanted to be there.

When she turned the knob to Firefly, the door swung open, revealing the muted gold walls and stone fireplace.

Renée gasped. "It's beautiful."

I handed her the towels. "I'll find some clothes and leave them on the bed for you."

She was too enamored with the room to focus on me. "Thanks."

I closed the door and hurried down to the master suite. The man who had lived here after Esme died had boxed up all of her clothes. And, until now, I didn't need to go through them. But from the pictures I had of Esme, she and Renée seemed to be of similar size.

As if I'd wished for it, the perfect cozy outfit sat right at the top of the first box I opened. I brought the clothes to my nose and smelled the lilac scent that often made its way down the halls. Even though I never met Esme, I imagined this was how she smelled.

I returned to Firefly knocking before walking in.

"The clothes are on the bed," I said, but Renée probably couldn't hear me over the sound of the shower.

She'd taken her clothes off right in the middle of the floor. I picked them up and went to knock on the bathroom door to ask whether she wanted me to wash them, but then thought better of it.

Instead, I took them back to the laundry area and

quickly went through them. The pant legs were singed at the bottoms and torn in the shins. A scarf shoved into the jacket pocket had specks of what looked like dried blood on it. And her shirt smelled like she hadn't changed her clothes in weeks.

I left them on top of the washer and closed the door.

The water in the bathroom turned off, leaving space for Renée's lovely singing that meandered down the hall-way. I was ninety-nine percent certain she was singing in Spanish.

I tip-toed down the stairs and went to the kitchen to make hot cocoa.

But first, I needed to call Deb.

"What did you do with my clothes?" Renée asked as I handed her a mug of hot cocoa.

"I put them in the wash," I said. "They were pretty bad."

"You try surviving outside in the cold." She sipped her cocoa and closed her eyes.

"What do you mean? You couldn't have been living outside."

"Well, not living, no," she said. "More like running."

"From who?"

"Whoever sent me those letters."

"What did the other letters say?" I asked before taking a sip of my own hot cocoa. It wasn't as good as hers, but it warmed me up and made me sleepy.

"Some of them asked for me to give them what they wanted. Others threatened to kill me."

"Did they have your name on them?"

"No." She sighed. "But they were in all the places I would look. My vanity. The icebox. My car. If they would have been trying to threaten Clancy, don't you think they would have put them where Clancy would have found them?"

She had a point.

"Who do you think wanted something, and what did they want?"

"It could be anyone. And I think it's pretty obvious what they want. They want my money. But they won't get it. Clancy will defend it with his life."

I sucked in a breath. "When did you leave your house?"

"The night after our last session." She took another sip, leaving a bit of chocolate foam on her upper lip, which she licked off with the tip of her tongue. "I found a bunch of notes and freaked."

"Have you talked to Clancy? Did you tell him where you went?"

She shook her head. "I thought it would be best to leave my phone at home so it couldn't be tracked."

"Except you've been texting me all week about being at the class on Saturday." I pulled out my phone and showed her the texts.

"I didn't send those."

"Then who did?"

"Clancy's the only person other than me who knows my passcode. Maybe he did."

"But why would he have acted like everything was okay?" I asked. "Especially if you were gone?"

She glanced down into her mug.

"What aren't you telling me?"

"It was a stupid idea," she said, still not looking up at

me. "I didn't want him to worry, so I wrote him a note that told him I left him for Weston and not to come looking for me."

"You what?" I could feel my jaw drop open.

"I got to thinking about what we talked about and how I couldn't ever cheat on Clancy. But then with my life being threatened, I figured I might as well live the way I wanted to."

"And did you tell Weston about your idea?"

She glanced up with tears in her eyes. "I didn't have time to," she said.

"Why not?"

"Because I was running for my life." She enunciated every syllable to make her point.

"From who, though? Who were you running from?"

"I don't know. That's what you're supposed to figure out, remember?" She took another sip. "But I can't go back to Clancy. Not now. He can have the money. Maybe they'll go after him instead of me. I might look like the easier target, but I'm tougher than I look. I mean, I almost died, my car was stolen, and I've been living in barns for days, but I'm still here. And I want to be with Weston."

There were so many things I needed to address, but before I could, Deb stepped into the room. "If only it were that easy."

"You called the police?" Renée stood.

"I had to," I said. "You were covered in blood."

"My blood," Renée said. "I thought we were friends."

"Ellie was doing what we've asked her to do—call the police when things might be dangerous."

"I'm really sorry about back there in the barn. I would

never have hurt your pig. I was just afraid." Renée took another step backward, bumping into a wall.

"What happened?" I asked. "If that blood was yours, how did it get all over you? Did someone attack you? Did you get a good look at them?"

"No one attacked me," Renée said. "There was a rabbit in the middle of the road the night I left my house. I didn't have my lights on. I saw it too late."

Deb looked like she was already tired of this story. That or she didn't believe a word of it.

"I got out and tried to see if it was okay, but it hopped away." Renée waited a few seconds for us to say something. When we didn't, she continued, "Well, I thought it was pretty miraculous. Anyway, I was walking back to the driver's side of my car when my headlights turned on and practically blinded me. I heard the car go into gear and realized it was driving right toward me. I only had a split-second to jump into the ditch, or it would have hit me. Unfortunately, the ditch was more like a cliff. I'm just lucky I didn't hit my head on the rocks on the way down."

She lifted her pant legs and then rolled up her sleeves. "See?"

"And where were you earlier this evening?" Deb checked her watch. "Or rather, yesterday evening?"

"I was on my way here," Renée said. "I was convinced Ellie had something to do with the threatening notes. Clancy got all in my head about her trying to swindle me with her exercises and everything. I'm really sorry. I swear, I wouldn't have hurt Ellie or Penelope."

I felt terrible for calling Deb. But if there was even the

slightest chance Renée had something to do with Clancy's death, calling Deb was the right thing to do.

"Unfortunately," Deb said. "Until we can determine whether that blood is, in fact, yours, I have to take you down to the station."

"Well, I don't want to go," Renée said. "I know my rights. If you're not arresting me, I don't have to go to the station."

Deb pulled out her handcuffs and showed them to Renée. "If you'd please put your hands behind your back."

"You're arresting me for being bloody?" Renée looked like we were about to tell her this was a big practical joke. "Why? What do you think I did? Kill someone?"

It was then I realized if Renée's story was true, she wouldn't have known that Clancy was dead.

"Deb, hold on," I said. "Can I talk to you for a minute?"

"After I handcuff her," Deb said.

Renée crossed her arms over her chest. Deb would have had her beat in any sort of physical challenge, but Renée had guts to stand up to Deb.

"Fine," Deb said. "But don't go anywhere."

"Penelope," I said. "Watch her."

Penelope had done nothing but watch Renée since we'd all congregated in the kitchen. It astonished me that Penelope had been caught by a woman in her mid-seventies but had practically chased a young witch off the premises. If only Penelope could talk. Maybe she'd tell me she knew Renée wasn't ever really going to hurt her.

"What is it?" Deb asked.

"Let's say Renée's telling the truth and her story's real."

Deb nodded.

"She wouldn't know yet that Clancy was dead, right?"

A smile turned the corners of Deb's mouth upward.

"But if she's faking it and she had something to do with Clancy's death," I said, "she's also faking not knowing."

"And she might slip up," Deb said.

"For now, arrest her for trespassing or breaking and entering or something," I said. "But wait to tell her about Clancy. She said she was leaving him, anyway."

"When?"

"Tonight," I said. "She left him a note that said she was running away to be with Weston."

"And then Clancy ends up dead, and Weston is standing over him," Deb whispered. "What if Clancy went after Weston first?"

I shrugged. "Maybe it would mean Weston was acting in self-defense?"

"Weston won't tell us anything," Deb said. "But maybe he will once his lawyer arrives. Thanks for the call. I have to admit it was a surprise."

"Why's that?"

"You always call Jake," she said. "Even tonight."

"I didn't know he was dating—or on a date," I said. "I'd already interrupted once. I figured I'd just call you since you were on duty."

"Makes sense," she said. "Georgia's nice. I think you'll like her if you give her a chance."

I didn't need Deb telling me how nice Jake's girlfriend

was. It didn't matter to me. He wasn't my dad. His dating life had no bearing on my life.

When I didn't respond, Deb walked back into the kitchen and proceeded to formally arrest Renée.

"You have to be kidding," Renée said. "I did nothing wrong other than hold a pig captive in a barn."

I didn't reply, and Deb simply kept reading Renée her Miranda rights.

"Are you still going to look for the person who sent those notes like you promised?" Renée asked me.

Deb looked over at me with surprise in her eyes.

"I'll see what I can do," I said.

After Deb deposited Renée into the back of her police car, she returned to bag Renée's clothes as evidence.

"Why don't you head to bed," Deb said. "I'll close your garage door for you."

"Thanks."

When she was gone, I locked all the doors and barely made it under the covers before falling into a deep sleep.

I t was a struggle to get out of bed only hours later, but Bex was short-staffed at the café and would definitely need my help.

Penelope reluctantly woke up so I could carry her down the stairs. If I left her upstairs, she would either go to the bathroom in the house or potentially hurt herself trying to go down the stairs. Pigs weren't exactly made to tackle stairs, especially the going down part.

"I'll see you later," I said. "Try to stay inside. It's supposed to be an extra cold day."

Whatever that meant. How it could get colder than it already was, I didn't know.

I bundled up in a hat, jacket, snow boots, gloves, and a scarf. Mona didn't normally break down, but I wasn't taking any chances.

When I pulled up to the café, the lights inside were on, and several cars were parked alongside the farmers' trucks.

I hurried in and started on my duties.

"Sorry, I'm a few minutes late," I said.

"From what I hear, you had quite the evening." Bex dropped off four mugs of coffee on a table. "I've already taken care of these four. Can you pick up those two tables and the farmers?"

I got to work. The farmers were easy. They had the same thing every day. The other two tables were full of guests I'd never seen in town before.

"Is there some sort of event going on this weekend that I missed?" I asked Bex as she walked by with plates from her hands up both arms.

"Help me deliver these?"

I hurried behind her and helped her hand out the plates to three separate tables and booths.

"Does it have to do with the pancakes?" I asked. Every single plate I'd handed out had a stack of three of the most delicious, crispy-edged pancakes expertly prepared by our two cooks.

"Haven't you heard?" Bex glanced at me as she headed back toward the kitchen to grab another order.

"Heard what?"

"Georgia Barnette wrote an article in some big food magazine about how we have the best crispy-edged pancakes in the Midwest."

"Is Georgia Barnette the same Georgia—"

"As Jake's girlfriend?" she finished.

I nodded.

"That's the one," Bex said. "And it looks like they just walked in. I'll let you have their table. She always leaves a massive tip."

Most of the town didn't know that Esme had left me a

sizable chunk of money along with the farm. Technically, I didn't have to work. But I enjoyed it.

I slapped a smile on my face and headed out to talk to Jake.

"Hi there," I said. "What can I get you?"

Jake and Georgia smiled up at me.

"Two stacks of those amazing pancakes, please," Georgia said.

"And two coffees," Jake said, shooting her an adoring smile.

"Will do," I said.

I started to walk away, but Jake said, "Ellie?"

I turned back. "Yeah?"

"I heard you went back to the crime scene last night. Wanna talk about it?"

All the tables were taken care of for the moment with full cups and plates. But Jake didn't need to know that.

"I'm slammed right now," I said. "But maybe another time?"

Jake looked around as if verifying my story. Irritation flowed through me that he was using his cop investigation stuff on me.

I didn't wait for him to reply but instead went and made myself look as busy as possible.

Once the rush died down, Bex and I got the chance to have our own breakfast.

"I can't believe how many people came in this morning," I said.

"I know," Bex said. "I've made more in tips this morning than I have all week. And it's all thanks to Georgia. She's going to put our town on the map."

I took a bite of pancake to keep my feelings from exiting my mouth.

"Ooh, why the sour look?" Bex said.

It was impossible to hide things from Bex. I'd never had a closer friend in my entire life. Even though sometimes it felt a bit claustrophobic or overwhelming, it mostly felt like real-life magic. The kind that existed without any actual magic but felt magical.

"You don't like her, do you?" Bex asked when I didn't reply.

I swallowed my bite and wiped my mouth with my napkin. "I don't even know her. I only found out about her last night."

"But they've been dating for weeks," Bex said. "Maybe even months."

"How do you know?"

"They come in here all the time."

"And you didn't think to tell me?"

Bex shook her head. "I didn't think it was a big deal."

"It's not," I said, but the shakiness in my voice gave me away.

"Is this because of your mom?"

The bells chimed, and before I could see who was coming through the door, I stood. "I'll get them."

"This conversation isn't over."

"It's not about my mom," I lied. "It's not about anything. I'm happy that he's happy. She seems really nice."

"Okay," Bex said in a voice that told me she didn't believe a word I'd just said.

But it didn't matter. She didn't have to believe me.

I grabbed a couple of menus from the stack, not seeing how many people sat in the booth toward the front. "Can I get you coffee or—oh, hi."

The man sitting in the booth was the same one who had asked for a rain check. The P.I. I'd completely forgotten about him.

"Sorry I had to run before," he said. "I have a rather pushy client. But he pays well, so I do what he tells me."

"It's no big deal," I said. "Do you want to try the pancakes again?"

"Definitely. And bacon and coffee too."

"Black coffee, right?"

"You remembered?" The dimple on his cheek made him even more adorable than he already was.

I shrugged. "I try."

"Is that the same guy that ditched his food the other day?" Bex asked when I got to the kitchen to put in his order.

"Yep," I said. "The P.I."

"Sounds like a match made in heaven. You like to investigate things, and so does he."

I laughed and poured his coffee.

"He's one of the cuter ones I've seen in Cliff Haven," Hank said from behind me. "One of you should definitely go for him."

Bex and I both laughed.

"He's not my type," Bex said. "But I think he'd look great with Ellie."

Hank nodded his agreement.

"You guys," I said, trying to keep my hair from changing. Unfortunately, that was nearly impossible.

"Oh look, we embarrassed her," Bex said, pointing to my newly blue hair.

I set the coffee down and pulled my hair into a tight bun. Thankfully, it had gotten shorter again overnight. I slipped a scarf over my hair to cover it up. The last thing I wanted was to freak out the P.I.

"You really shouldn't hide it from him," Bex said. "If he likes you, he'll be okay with your hair."

"I'll believe that when I see it." I'd lost more boyfriends than I could count because of my changing hair.

"You can't hide it forever," she sing-songed as I walked away to deliver his coffee.

"Nice scarf," he said.

"Thanks." I set the coffee down, and he took a sip.

"Mmmm," he said. "Good coffee."

"I'll be back when your food comes out." I started to leave but thought of something. "Any luck on the Baby—uh—"

"Bear," he said with a smile. "And a little bit, but the case isn't closed."

"Did you figure out who he was?"

He shrugged.

"Ah, right," I said. "Confidentiality."

He nodded, then glanced down at the file in front of him, open to a sheet that looked like a bank statement. He slowly closed the file so I couldn't peek.

"I understand." I felt completely awkward now. "Uh,

I'll be back with food." When I turned, I almost ran straight into Bex.

"Did Ellie tell you about her dance classes?" Bex asked.

"Ellie?" he said. "I like that. And no, Ellie did not tell me about said dance classes."

"There's one this evening," Bex said. "We're learning the tango."

"That's funny," he said. "I've always wanted to learn to tango."

Bex nudged me.

"You're welcome to come," I said. "We've only had one lesson so far."

"And if you have any friends, feel free to bring them too," Bex said. "I'm Bex, by the way."

"Kurt," he said. "I wish I had friends, but you're the first people I've met in town."

"Where are you from?" Bex asked.

"Here and there," Kurt said. "I go where my work takes me."

"Sounds adventurous," Bex said.

It would sound adventurous to someone who had lived their entire life in Cliff Haven, but I'd lived in the back of Mona for years, traveling all over the country. Though I made memories I wouldn't trade for anything, it also had its drawbacks.

"The flyer for the dance class is on the door," Bex said. "Feel free to stop by."

"I'll do that," he said, smiling at me.

My phone buzzed in my satchel as I was starting Mona. I was tired, smelled like bacon and coffee, and needed a nap and a shower before dance class.

I pulled out my phone to find Jake's name on the screen.

"Hello?"

"Hey," Jake said. "Have you left the café yet?"

"Just getting ready to," I said.

"Think you'd be able to stop by the station real quick before heading home? I promise I won't take too much of your time."

I wanted to say no. Avoid him forever. But I couldn't. "I'll be there in a couple of minutes."

The air was significantly colder today, just like my weather app had indicated. I didn't even bother turning on the heater because I knew it wouldn't get warm on the short drive.

"I'll be right back," I told Mona. "Then you can go back to your nice warm garage."

The police station was a small old building but had been updated inside fairly recently.

The receptionist waved and unlocked the door leading back to Jake's office when I walked in.

"Hey there," Jake said when I got to his office. "Want some coffee?"

I shook my head. "I'm planning on taking a nap before my lessons tonight."

"The dance ones?" His eyes lit up. "I just saw that on the café door. Do you have room for two more?"

"Sure," I said with a shrug.

"Is something wrong?" Jake asked.

I glanced at the cabinet behind his desk. He had replaced the photograph of him and my mother as teenagers with one of him and Georgia on what looked like a ski slope.

"Nope," I said, returning my gaze to him. "Just tired after last night."

"That's what I wanted to talk to you about," he said. "I heard you went back to find your purse in Renée's car."

"Uh, yeah," I said. I hated lying. Especially to those close to me.

"It's just that I've never heard you call it a purse before."

"Do you have a question for me?" I asked, knowing exactly what he was implying. And even though he was right, it still irked me.

"Did you make up an excuse to search her garage? And if so, how did you know there would be a clue out there?"

I didn't want to tell him I'd used my magic to track her. "I realized when we didn't find Renée that maybe she just took her car and left. I didn't think I'd find any clues —especially not a threatening note."

"Smart," he said. "We'd checked the garage too, but since there were so many cars in there, we didn't know whether one was missing. Is her car at your house now?"

I shook my head. "No. She said she walked to my house after she fell down the cliff and her car was stolen. Didn't Deb tell you?"

He shifted some papers on his desk. "I haven't had time to go through any of the notes. I only just got in when I called you." He seemed to find what he was looking for and held the piece of paper up. It looked like a photocopy of Deb's notebook.

"Let's see," he started reading down the page. "You called Deb . . . Renée had Penelope. Oh, I'm sorry. I didn't know." He looked up at me.

"It's okay. Penelope's fine."

He looked back down and kept reading. "Deb heard your conversation about what happened . . . the notes . . . the cliff . . . stolen car." He was quiet for a few seconds. "And she brought back bloody, torn, burned clothes. Those are being processed." He flipped the paper over. "Preliminary cause of death wasn't stabbing. Weston is set to be released today." He looked up at me. "Anything I'm missing?"

"Did they find anything on Clancy's phone?"

He looked back down at the paper. "I don't see anything about a phone."

"They had a security system. It was a bit wonky, but maybe it caught something."

"Cameras?" Jake asked.

I shrugged. "Not sure, but definitely motion detection and alerts. They went off several times when I was there for Renée's personal sessions."

"Did you see if something was tripping them up?"

"I looked almost every time," I said. "But it was probably just weird lighting or a bug or something."

"A bug in the middle of this winter?"

"Renée said it could have been a ghost."

"Probably more likely than a bug in this weather." He laughed.

I gaped at him. Not only did we have the same blue eyes and the same addiction to crispy-edged pancakes, we also thought a lot alike.

But he swore up and down he hadn't been with my mother in a way that could have gotten her pregnant.

"I'll follow up with the team about the phone," he said. "Anything else?"

"Does it say how Renée acted once she got here?"

He looked at the notes again. "I don't see anything."

"When does Deb get in?"

"She was here all morning, so I suspect not until later. Why?"

"I'm surprised she didn't leave it in her notes," I said. "But she and I agreed not to tell Renée that Clancy was dead."

He sat back in his chair and studied me. Finally, he said, "Makes sense. If she did it, she'd have to act like she didn't know. But if she didn't, her actions might tell us that, right?"

"Exactly." I exhaled, relieved he wasn't angry. "And I wanted to see if she'd done anything."

"I'll call down to the jail and see if they have any notes on it." He picked up the phone and dialed three numbers. "Hi, it's Jake. Are there any notes from last night about Renée's behavior?" He paused. "Ah, okay. Yep. I'll look. Thanks."

He put the phone back in its cradle and turned to his computer screen. "They sent me the shift notes an hour ago."

"Are you doing okay?" I asked.

"I'm great," Jake said, frowning. "Georgia has convinced me to leave my work at work so I can more thoroughly enjoy my time off."

"I bet she was mad that you got called out of your date last night."

He turned from his computer to face me. "Actually, she wasn't. She's really understanding about things. She gets that I have to be on call all the time, but has also taught me that there's more to life than work."

He turned back to the screen. I slouched a bit in my chair. If Emily was alive, she needed to come back before it was too late.

The idea hit me almost too hard. It was so obvious. If I could use my magic to locate Renée, I could use my magic to locate Emily. I mean, sure, Esme hadn't had any luck. But that didn't mean I shouldn't try.

"Here it is," Jake said. "They booked Renée and gave

her the chance for a phone call. First, she called Weston, who didn't answer since he was in jail."

I was only half-listening. I needed to get home so I could try to find my mom.

"Then she called her attorney." He paused, scanning down the screen. "That's about it. She hasn't said anything at the advice of her lawyer." Jake glanced up at me. "That could mean she knows Clancy's dead."

"Or maybe not," I said. "She left him a note saying she didn't want to be with him anymore. I'm guessing she won't go back on that even if she is in jail."

"Do you want to try to talk to her?" Jake asked. "She can have visitors."

"I don't think she'll say much to me. Especially after I basically set her up last night."

"You could try."

I didn't want to try. This was not a case I wanted to involve myself in. Clancy was dead, and one of my friends was the most viable suspect.

But I couldn't let Jake down. Even if I was irritated.

I glanced back at the picture of the woman who was pushing my mother out of Jake's heart. He deserved to be happy. I wanted him to be happy. And if I couldn't find Emily, then I needed to accept that he would move on—whether it was with Georgia or someone else.

Honestly, it was a surprise he hadn't moved on before now.

"I'll try," I finally said. "But let's make it quick. I'm exhausted from last night, and I have to be ready for dance class."

Within minutes, I was in the visitation room, waiting for Renée to appear. Part of me hoped she wouldn't.

But when she walked in, my heart felt heavy.

She looked miserable.

"I didn't think anyone would come to visit me," she said after sitting across the glass from me and picking up the phone.

"Why not?" I asked into my phone. On the glass, large signs stated that phone calls were recorded.

"I don't know," she said. "Weston didn't answer my call, my lawyer acted strangely when I called him, and even though I left Clancy that note, I thought he'd still come. He always said he loved me no matter what."

"You thought he'd visit even though you left him that note and used your one call to call Weston and your attorney instead of him?" I asked.

"It sounds stupid." She wiped a tear from the corner of her eye. "But we've been together so long. I didn't think he'd dismiss me so easily. Even after all this."

I didn't know what to say to her. I was fairly certain I wasn't supposed to tell her Clancy was dead, but it really seemed like she didn't know.

"Maybe he's busy," I said.

Her eyes widened. "Or maybe he's on the run too." She sat forward, a newfound determination on her face. "Whoever was after me is probably after him now. They want our money, and they'll do anything to get it."

"Who is they?" I asked.

"I thought you were trying to figure that out."

"I—uh—I am."

"Please," she said. "I know I said I want to be with

Weston, but I changed my mind. Clancy would have never ignored my call. I should have called him." She looked at the door behind me. "Maybe you can convince them to let me have another call. He'll get me out of here."

"I'll see what I can do," I said.

"Thank you." Renée sat back. "I know I said it yesterday, but I'm very sorry I came after you and your piggy. I shouldn't have let Clancy's paranoia about you get to me. If he takes me back, I promise I'll let him know he doesn't need to worry about you."

I could hardly smile. "It's okay. I'll talk to the officers and see about getting you that phone call. Keep doing your exercises in there so you're ready to go to Argentina, okay?"

"I will," she said. "Thank you so much."

She would hate me when she found out I knew Clancy was dead the entire time.

I nearly walked right into Deb when I yanked open the door out of the visitation room.

"We have to—"

Deb held up a hand. "I know," she said. "Do you want me to do it, or do you want to be there too?"

Everything in me wanted to just let Deb do it. But that wouldn't be right. I needed to own up to it. Face Renée head-on. Even if it meant I lost a friend in the long run.

I turned back to see Renée still sitting in the chair, looking down into her lap, almost as if she was praying.

Deb tapped on the glass, and Renée's head shot up. She mouthed the words, "I'm not talking to you," and pointed at Deb.

I picked up the phone receiver. Renée did the same.

"There's something I need to tell you." I glanced at Deb, who nodded.

"Oh no," she said. "What is it?"

"Clancy died," I said as gently as I could.

She gasped, clapping a hand over her mouth. The

phone receiver fell out of her hand as tears welled up in her eyes.

The guard on Renée's side of the glass put a tissue box on the counter in front of her, but she seemed to be in shock.

"Renée?" I said into the phone, not sure if she could still hear me. "There's more to the story. I'd like to tell you when you're ready."

It seemed to take hours for her to reach for the phone dangling from its cord. "Did you say something?" She asked. Her eyes were glazed over, almost as if she was in a trance, but at least I knew she could hear me now. I needed to get this all out in the open.

"Clancy didn't just die," I said. "It looks like someone murdered him."

This brought the focus back into her eyes as her gaze landed on me. "What do you mean, someone murdered him?"

"The other night when I went looking for you—before I found you in my barn—I found him at your house."

"You knew this entire time and didn't tell me?"

"I'm sorry," I said. "We wanted to see if perhaps you were responsible for his death."

"Me?" Her voice was growing increasingly irritated. "You thought I killed Clancy?"

"We didn't know," I said. "You were in my barn, threatening Penelope and me, covered in blood."

"My own blood. Test it," Renée said. "It's not Clancy's blood."

"I'm sure it's being tested as we speak," I said. "But here's the thing—we need to know who might have done this. And why? Your house was completely ransacked. Every single room."

Renée's face paled even further. "What do you mean my house was ransacked?"

"It seemed like someone was looking for something," I said. "Do you know what that could have been?"

"Money, probably," she said. "But they wouldn't have found any. Not in the house."

"If you didn't keep it in the house, where did you keep it?" If it was in a barn or a shed or something, we probably needed to make sure it was secure.

"In a bank," she said. "Where else would I keep it?"

I almost laughed at myself but figured it wasn't the most appropriate thing to do. "Right."

"But someone might have thought we kept it in the house. I mean, there were valuables at the house—jewelry and such—they could have stollen those."

I glanced back at Deb. "Were any valuables taken? I don't remember."

Deb shrugged. "From what we could tell, the electronics and jewelry all seemed to be there. But we'll need to get a formal inventory from Renée before we can be certain."

"If the jewelry was there," Renée said. "Then I have no idea what they were looking for. Maybe if I'm released, I can go back to the house and tell you if anything is missing."

"She said maybe if she's released, she can go back to the house to see if she can determine if anything's missing," I said.

Deb shook her head, and Renée slumped back in her chair. "I don't know how I can help you from in here."

"I guess, if you think of anything, you can let Deb know?" I said.

"Right," Renée said.

"Oh," I said. "One more thing. Can you give us the passcode to Clancy's phone?"

"You or them?" She looked at Deb.

"Uh, well, both of us, I guess."

She crossed her arms over her chest. "You know, I don't think I remember his passcode."

Deb leaned down and whispered in my ear, "If we find the phone, we can get a warrant, but unless we have a passcode, we're dead in the water."

"How about if you remember it, you give it to me, and I promise to talk to you about anything I want to share with the police before I share it?" I asked.

I could feel Deb tense up when I said this.

"What is it you think you'll find?" Renée asked.

"The biggest thing we want to check is the footage and records from the alarm system," I said.

"That's on my phone, too. I definitely remember my passcode."

"The problem is, we haven't been able to locate your phone."

"I left it in the nightstand next to my bed," she said. "The passcode is one-two-three-four but don't tell her."

I glanced back at Deb. If I remembered correctly, their bedroom had been completely ransacked.

Deb gave me a questioning look since she couldn't hear what Renée had just told me.

I turned back to Renée. "If we find it, there could be additional evidence on Clancy's phone. So if you remember the passcode, have Deb call me."

She nodded and hung the phone up without so much as a goodbye. I hung up my receiver and waved before I followed Deb out of the room.

"You shouldn't have given her that deal," Deb said. "Once that phone is unlocked, the warrant will take over, and everything on it will be police evidence."

"Then I guess she'll never remember the code," I said, walking past her toward the exit doors.

Deb huffed and followed behind me. "Fine. Fine. We can do it your way. But if you see something important on that phone and she tells you not to tell us, then what?"

I considered this. I'd already lied to Renée once. I really didn't want to break her trust again. "I don't know."

"Think about it before you get yourself into this because if you don't think you'll be able to tell us, that could jeopardize the case."

She was right, but I was tired and stinky and I wanted to get home to try to locate my mother.

"I'll think about it." I started out the door but turned back around. "She gave me the code to her phone—not that I'm going to share it," I added quickly. "But if you find it, I could help you access it."

"Any idea where it might be?" Deb was visibly frustrated with me.

"In her nightstand," I said.

Deb rubbed a hand over her face in obvious irritation. "The bedroom was destroyed, but we'll take another look."

Mona seemed only too happy to start up and head home. Mona was the only vehicle I'd owned. I'd bought her when I turned sixteen and ran away from my last foster family. And not once did I ever consider getting a new vehicle. Even though seat heaters would have been pretty nice.

When I turned onto the main road that led through town and toward my house, I noticed an overly fancy car at the gas station. It wasn't a car I'd seen in town before, so I peeked over to see who was driving. One person sat behind the wheel while another pumped gas. But that person wasn't pumping gas into the car's tank but into a gas can. And on second look, I did recognize the man pumping gas. It was Weston.

Part of me wanted to pull in and see what was going on—talk to him about the case. But a bigger part of me wanted to get home. If the police released him, they obviously thought he didn't do it, so there was no reason to keep harassing him.

The garage was warm when I pulled in, and I could almost feel Mona sigh in relief when I closed the door, encasing her in the cozy atmosphere. Her pink paint job with the words Relief with Ellie on the side was starting to fade. I'd have to repaint her this summer. Maybe with a couple of big daisies.

Penelope was curled up in her bed in the living room but looked up when she saw me walk in.

"How was your day?" I leaned down and kissed her on top of the head. "Hopefully, less eventful than yesterday."

She seemed less affected by yesterday's events than I was. But she was a tough little piggy.

"I'm going to go try to use my magic."

This perked her up. She trotted along behind me to the kitchen island, where I thought I'd give it a go.

My eyes were heavy, but I knew I wouldn't be able to sleep without at least trying to find my mother.

I focused on the countertop in front of me and thought about her name in my head.

Emily Vanderwick.

I closed my eyes and instantly felt my hair changing. The picture in my mind's eye was dark with a pinpoint of light. Or, perhaps, a speck of magic.

I clung to the speck. Followed the light.

Is she alive? Is Emily alive?

I focused on the question, waiting for a feeling.

The speck grew, illuminating the surroundings.

A hum in the air started as low as the whirring of a fan but grew until it sounded more like a freight train.

The speck was coming at me.

Fast.

I was trapped underground.

The surrounding scene came into focus.

It was a tunnel.

And the train was real.

My feet were heavy.

I couldn't move.

It was going to hit me.

I squeezed my eyes shut tighter, then remembered it was only a vision.

When I opened my eyes, dizziness washed over me.

I fell to my hands and knees, trying to focus on the floor.

Penelope was at my side, nudging me with her nose. Her faint oinks asking if I was okay.

"I'm fine," I said. "I'm okay."

I sucked in a breath and tried to steady myself.

Though my vision was blurry, two things were clear:

My mother was alive.

And in grave danger.

<hr>

I didn't have the ability to sleep. I had to help my mom. But how?

I paced my bedroom until my legs grew so heavy, I had to sit. How I fell asleep was a mystery to me, but when I woke, I felt like I hadn't slept in weeks. My body was exhausted, but my mind was like gelatin.

And my hair—oh my hair. It was so short now—shorter than I could remember it ever being. It hung gray and lifeless just below my earlobes.

I combed it out, slipped on some comfy leggings and an oversized sweatshirt, and called it good.

Penelope and I made our way to the barn, her not taking her eyes off me. Who knew using magic could be so draining?

Everything was still where it needed to be for class. The only thing Renée had disrupted was the curtain.

When I went to pull it back into place, I noticed a change in the painting.

I'd almost gotten out of the habit of looking at it since it hadn't changed in so long. But the change was so dramatic, it would have been impossible to miss.

The painting had always been of the farm. The people changed, but the backdrop didn't.

Until now.

"Whoa, what happened here?" Xander asked, coming up next to me.

I shook my head. "It . . . changed."

"Are you okay?" Xander asked. "You don't look well."

"I used my magic."

A heavy silence filled the space between us.

There were still no people in the painting, and my mother's signature remained at the bottom of the page.

"How did you use your magic?" Xander finally asked.

"I wanted to find her," I said. "It worked for Renée, so I thought it would work for Emily too."

Xander grabbed me by the shoulders and spun me so I was facing him. "You tried to find Emily? With your magic?"

I nodded, unable to be as excited as he seemed to be.

Or maybe he was angry. I couldn't tell. My brain still felt like goo.

"She's alive," I said. "But I think she's in trouble."

"How? What . . ?" Xander took a deep breath. "How did you figure this out?"

"I just closed my eyes and focused. I found the edges of the magic and focused."

"And you saw your mother in trouble but alive?"

I shook my head. "Not exactly."

"Then what? What did you see?"

"That." I pointed to the mural. "I saw that."

"You saw a train in a tunnel?"

"I was in the tunnel. Trapped. My feet wouldn't move. I think I was Emily. Or a representation of what Emily's feeling right now. I don't know. It was more of an intuitive thing. And then I came out here, and the mural changed. There's no more farm."

Xander pulled me into his arms, and it was only at this point I realized I was crying.

"It's okay," he said. "Sometimes magic is confusing."

"Harriet was right. He has her held captive," I said. "Our cousin. That has to be it. He took away her magic so he could have our grandfather's inheritance."

"Do you know this for sure?" Xander asked, his hand holding my head to his chest.

"Not for sure, but it makes sense, right?"

"If what Harriet was telling was the truth, then yes," Xander said. "But she may not know. She seemed to be making an educated guess."

"Well, if it's not my cousin who has Emily, it's someone else. She's trapped. Her magic is trapped. And we need to help her." I pulled back and looked up into his eyes, trying not to get dizzy again. "When I feel better, I'll try again. Maybe I'll get more information."

"It's not safe, El." He looked down at me with those big green eyes filled with worry. "You tried once, and you look like you're on death's doorstep."

"I just have to exercise my magic more," I said, pulling away. "Or you could help me."

"I can't do magical tracing," he said. "If I could, I would have already found her by now."

"Then let's find someone who can," I said. "Another witch or wizard."

"The last witch or wizard known to be able to track another witch or wizard was your grandmother."

I gaped at him. "There has to be someone else. Maybe they just don't know they can."

He shook his head.

I squared my shoulders. "Then it's up to me. I'll try again. Soon."

"Penelope, would you talk some sense into her?" Xander asked.

I looked at Penelope, who just stood at our feet, looking up at the mural.

"I'm perfectly sensible," I said. "Sure, my mind and body feel pretty rough right now, but using my magic like that was probably like running a marathon with no training. If I continually use my magic in more and more difficult ways, I'll be able to track my mother fully."

Xander didn't seem to like that idea much, but the door to the barn opened, and people started flooding in.

"We can talk about it later," I said and walked away to greet my friends.

The swell of laughter and chit-chat inside the barn warmed my heart.

"Is everyone ready?" I asked.

Jake and Georgia held hands toward the back by Katie and Earl. Nancy and Hank were next to Amy and Fran. And Bex and Laura stood off to the side.

"Am I late?" a voice came from the door.

I turned to see Kurt walking through the door. "Not at all," I said.

Laura nudged Bex, but Bex leaned over and said something in her ear that made Laura's face go sour.

"How about we do a bit of a refresh of the steps from last class so the newbies can catch up?" I said.

"I want another demonstration," Nancy said.

"Not this time," Xander said, walking over to stand by Laura. Her face went from sour to sweet in an instant.

Unfortunately, his rejection turned my stomach a bit sour.

Kurt walked to stand by Bex, and I started with the basic steps.

Everyone seemed to remember, and Jake and Georgia were quick learners.

Kurt, on the other hand, seemed lost.

Bex was trying to help him, but she had only just gotten the steps herself.

As everyone continued, I walked over and helped him.

"I've never been good at dancing," he said, rubbing the back of his neck.

"That's okay," I said. "Here, let's start from the beginning."

I placed my hand on his arm and helped move him through the motions.

"There," I said. "You're getting it."

He smiled at me. "You're a great teacher."

I could feel Xander's eyes on us, but I didn't care. He and I were friends. Nothing more. I could flirt with anyone I wanted to.

The class went on, and eventually, everyone paired up and started trying the steps together.

I watched as each of the couples danced together, offering guidance as necessary. I mostly stayed away from Xander and Laura. He didn't need my guidance, and—from the looks of things—he and Laura worked surprisingly well together.

Laura and I had been on better terms than when I'd first moved to Cliff Haven, but her family was fully against magic. Just because she was nice to me didn't mean she liked me.

But she definitely seemed to like Xander.

I mean, what wasn't to like?

He was intriguing, sexy, and funny in his own dry way.

I guess she was only against magic when it came to witches.

But what irked me even more was that Xander actually seemed to enjoy her company.

"You okay?" Kurt asked, walking up next to me.

"I'm great," I said, my voice almost too perky.

"Bex needed to get a drink of water and suggested I ask you to dance." He almost seemed shy, which wasn't exactly what I expected from a P.I. But it was cute.

"I'd love to dance," I said.

He wasn't as skilled as Xander, but at least he didn't step on my feet.

"How do you do it?" He asked.

"Do what?"

"Dance like you're gliding on air?" He looked down at our feet. "I feel so clompy."

"Practice," I said. I didn't add that it was probably partially to do with my magic. I seemed to be extra good at most physical things. Like bowling—I hadn't bowled in ages, and a few months ago, I bowled the perfect game.

"I like your hair," he said. "Did you dye it today?"

Normally, I would have said yes. I would have lied. Because that's what he expected. But I didn't want to start . . . whatever this was . . . with a lie.

"It's magic," I said. "I'm a witch."

He stopped dancing for a second. I thought he might either storm out or start laughing, but instead, he nodded. "That's cool."

It was my turn to stop in my tracks. "Really?"

"Really. It's not like you're the first witch I've ever met." He pulled me closer, and we started dancing again. I wanted to ask him about his statement but decided to simply enjoy dancing.

Bex gave me a questioning look. I responded with a thumbs-up behind Kurt's back.

"Can I take you out sometime?" Kurt asked. "I'm not sure how long I'll be in town, but I like you."

"I think we can arrange that."

"How about after class? Are you busy?"

Technically, I owed Xander dinner and a movie, but he didn't seem too keen on me right now. "Nope. I'll just have to change into something warmer." And cuter. And put on makeup. And maybe try to fix my hair.

"No problem," he said.

The alarm on my phone went off, signaling the end of class.

"Thank you all for coming tonight," I said, stepping back from Kurt. "You've all improved leaps and bounds."

"Next time, will you teach us that fancy lift thing you and Xander did?" Amy asked in her gravelly voice.

I shook my head. "I think we need a few more basic classes first."

Xander and Laura had been slow to separate. And now they were talking in whispers with their heads nearly touching.

Jealousy rose within me, and I could feel my scalp tingle.

"Oh wow," Kurt said beside me. "You weren't lying. You are a witch."

Usually, when people called me a witch, they were saying it in a derogatory way. But his words were kind.

I shrugged. "I wish I could control it."

"Why does it change?"

"Typically, my moods dictate the color and texture," I said.

"And what mood does green signify?"

I didn't want to lie to him, but I couldn't tell him the real reason my hair had turned green.

I shrugged. "Sometimes, I don't know."

"It's fascinating," he said.

"I'm going to head inside and get ready," I said. "I'll see everyone next weekend."

Several people yelled out their goodbyes as I walked out the door.

Within fifteen minutes, I was ready to go. I pulled on my magical jacket and headed back out to the barn, where Penelope and Kurt stood awkwardly.

"Ready?" I asked.

"Is this your friend?" He pointed to Penelope.

"Yep," I said. "That's Penelope."

"She's a tough one," he said. "Kept an eye on me the entire time."

"She's been through a lot lately." I picked her up and snuggled her.

"Poor little piggy." He reached out to pet her head, but she snapped at him and squealed.

He yanked his hand back, his eyes wide.

"I'll just take her inside and meet you at your car, okay?"

We walked out of the barn, and I locked it behind me.

When he was out of earshot, I whispered to Penelope, "What was that? Kurt's nice. Are you doing okay?"

She wiggled her nose against my cheek as if trying to reassure me.

"I'll be home early," I said. "Stay inside unless you have to use the bathroom, okay? It's freezing."

I deposited her inside the back door and locked it. Of course, if anyone wanted to get in, they could try to get through the piggy door. But the house's magical protections usually kept dangerous people away.

This thought stopped me in my tracks. It usually kept dangerous people away, but Renée had gotten into the barn. And had been permitted into one of the rooms to shower.

I wanted to call and tell Deb about this, but what would I say? My house thinks Renée is innocent? She'd die laughing at me.

I shook my head. I didn't need to think about this right now. I was going on a date and would have a good time.

When I slipped into the front seat of Kurt's little car, I couldn't help but notice all the stuff. The entire back seat was covered in sporting equipment and fishing equipment and cases of files. Bottles of water and soda filled the cup holders, and a few pieces of stray trash littered the floorboards.

"Sorry about the mess," he said. "I didn't expect to go on a date."

I laughed. "It's no problem. So, where are we off to?"

"There's a casino a couple of towns over. I thought it might be fun to try our luck."

I'd never been gambling before. Usually when I traveled, I had Penelope with me and a minimal budget. I couldn't just leave her inside Mona while I tested my luck with our gas and food money. But now, my expendable income was slightly more.

"Sounds fun," I said.

He backed out of the driveway and onto the gravel road. "Your friends are nice."

"They're pretty awesome," I agreed.

"Xander seemed a bit taken aback that I was taking you on a date," he said, not taking his eyes off the road. "Is there a history between the two of you?"

"No," I said. "We're just friends."

He stopped at the stop sign that led to the main road. A car coming toward us had its blinker on. Kurt waited for it to turn before pulling out. Which made sense because the other car wasn't slowing down.

"Kurt?" was all I could get out before the other car smashed into us.

17

"Ellie?" Kurt's voice came from the passenger seat. Surprisingly, I felt fine. "I'm okay," I said. "Are you?"

"I'm okay," he said, pushing his airbag back toward the steering wheel.

"We should check on the other driver," I said, opening my door.

"I don't think my door will open."

"Can you climb through this way?"

He shimmied over the center console and into my seat.

"Can you call 9-1-1?" I asked before heading toward the car.

If Kurt's car was an apartment in Cliff Haven, the other one would have been a mansion in Malibu.

The driver seemed to be unconscious when I walked to the window. I could hardly see in with the dark tint and tried to open the door, but it was still locked.

I tapped and saw some movement.

"Can you unlock the door?" I yelled.

Kurt was on the phone with dispatch behind me.

The doors unlocked, and I opened the driver's door carefully.

The man in the driver's seat had a cut on his head and was cradling one arm in his other.

"I'm Ellie," I said. "Are you okay?"

"I think my arm's broken," he said. "And my stomach hurts."

"Do you mind if I touch you?" I'd used my magic to help people get relief. At first, I hadn't known that my touch had those types of powers. But as my clients grew in number, I frequently noticed they achieved their goals more quickly than was physically possible.

"Feel free," the man said. He wore an expensive suit and had a nicely maintained beard.

I placed a hand on his shoulder and concentrated.

Pain radiated up my arm.

That was another part of the magic—sometimes, I felt overwhelming feelings the other person was experiencing.

If I was feeling his pain, he had to be in more of it than he let on.

I concentrated and felt the pain receding back down my arm. How far my magic could go was unclear. I'd never tried to bring relief to someone with broken bones or possible internal bleeding.

"Why didn't you stop?" I asked when his breathing became more normal.

"I didn't see you," he said. "Your car must have blended into the snowbank. I took the corner too fast and lost control of my steering. I'm so sorry. Is everyone okay?"

"We're fine," I said.

Behind me, Kurt sounded like he was on the phone with his insurance. "But the cars are both pretty damaged."

"Did you call the police?" he asked.

"We did," I said. "Is that a problem?"

"Yes," he said. "And no."

I didn't need to get in his business, but I didn't have to ask for him to start talking.

"I was cheating on my wife tonight. If she finds out I got in an accident here, looking like this, she'll know."

I took my hand off his shoulder. If there was something I hated, it was people who lied. And if the transfer of emotion went the other way, he would have instantly felt my disdain for him.

"I'm sorry," he said again. "I shouldn't have said anything. It's my problem, not yours."

The lights of the police car shone behind me as it approached.

"Are you feeling any better?" I asked.

He moved his arm and pushed on his stomach. "Much," he said, then looked up at me with fear in his eyes. "What did you do?"

"Nothing," I said. "Sometimes human touch is all people need. Maybe you should try it on your wife."

I turned and let the paramedics deal with him. Frustration with myself seeped over me. I shouldn't treat anyone with such disrespect. I didn't know his situation.

I turned back and said, "I'm sorry. Please excuse my rudeness."

He smiled. "I deserved it."

A hand rested on my shoulder. "A rental car will be here shortly," Kurt said. "We could still go to the casino if you want to."

I was shaken, but I couldn't let every little thing keep me from going on a date. Sure, a murder differed from a car accident, but Xander would be around for a while. Kurt might not be. This might be my only chance to get to know him. It wasn't every day a guy accepted that my hair was magical.

"I'm up for it."

His face lit up. "Perfect."

The officers who showed up were ones I didn't know. They gave the guy in the fancy car a breathalyzer, and apparently, he came back clear.

"Did he say why he hit us?" Kurt asked.

"He said he didn't see us—that the car blended into the snow." I looked over at the smashed-up car and realized it was possible. The snow and the car were both the same color, after all. "And he was going too fast and lost steering when he started sliding."

Kurt looked over, and the two men made eye contact.

"Hey, don't I know you?" the man asked.

Kurt turned away. "Don't think so."

The paramedics helped the man into the back of the ambulance, but the whole time he stared at the back of Kurt's head as if trying to place him.

"What's that all about?"

"His wife is one of my clients," Kurt said. "He's cheating on her."

That made sense. "Yes, he is. He told me so."

"He told you?" Kurt's eyes widened.

"Plain as day," I said. "When I told him we called the police."

"Because she'll find out," Kurt said, then let out a curse word.

"What?"

"If she finds out because of this, I won't get payment," he said.

"Then call her," I said. "I'll tell her what he told me."

Kurt's eyes lit up. "Would you?"

"Sure," I said.

He pulled his phone out of his pocket and tapped the screen before holding it up to his ear. "Hi, it's Kurt. I have information for you." He paused. "I'd like to have you speak with my associate. She spoke with your husband tonight."

He handed me the phone. "Hello?"

Her voice was tired on the other side. "What did he say?"

"Your husband was in a car accident near Cliff Haven just a few minutes ago. I was one of the first on scene. When I checked on him, he was worried I'd call the police."

She sucked in a breath.

"Then he told me he was cheating on you, and if you knew where he'd gotten in the accident, you'd immediately know."

There was only silence on the other end of the line.

"Are you still there?"

"He's going to wish that accident killed him. Can I talk to Kurt again?"

I handed the phone back to Kurt, worried about what

I'd just done. Was she going to finish the job? Would I have another murder on my hands?

"Take a breath," Kurt said. "You already suspected this was the case. Now you have proof. Remember the contingency plan you put together? Now is the time to enact it."

He nodded at whatever she was saying.

"That sounds great," he said. "And if you could just wire that money tonight, that would be great."

He hung up with a smile on his face.

"You don't think she'll actually kill him, do you?" I asked.

"Not a chance," Kurt said. "But she will take most of his money."

His phone chimed, and he showed me the screen and an absurd number preceded by a dollar sign. "That deserves a celebration."

18

A rental car was delivered within the hour.

"Can you help me get everything transferred from my car?"

He handed me a couple of file boxes while he grabbed the various balls and bats and gloves.

"Do you coach baseball or something?" I asked.

He glanced down at the things in his arms. "My nephews like to play. I keep it with me for when I'm passing through town. We'll play a game or two."

That might have been the sweetest thing I'd ever heard. "Do they like to fish too?"

He glanced at the small tackle box and fishing rod in the back seat. "Nope, that's all me."

I put the box in the back of the rental car and went back for more.

Several pieces of paper, blurry photographs, and what looked like the shattered pieces of a broken cell phone were scattered all over the back seat. I gathered the photographs until one caught my eye—Renée and Clancy's house.

"Oh hey," Kurt said. "I'll grab those. Confidentiality and all."

Him and his confidentiality.

I tried to take one more look at the picture of the house but couldn't determine whether it was theirs. "Is this around here?"

Kurt inspected the photo. "That one?" He thought about it for a second. "I think that one is in Indiana. Why?"

"It looks like a friend of mine's house," I said. "I thought maybe you were investigating her."

He laughed. "I'm not currently investigating any women. And this house belonged to an elderly couple. Sadly, they've since passed away."

I grabbed the fishing rod and the relatively light tackle box and put them in the back of the rental car. "Did you have a mishap with your cell phone?" I pointed to the pieces he was depositing into the box with the photographs.

"I'm so hard on things," he said. "It's a good thing they offer insurance. Ready to go?"

"Yep."

He handed his keys to the tow truck driver and we hopped into the rental car.

The drive to the casino was filled with small talk. Kurt gushed about his nephews and asked about my family. I gave him an overview. I didn't need to bring the mood down talking about how my mother abandoned me and my grandmother had died before I met her.

No way. Tonight would be fun.

"Earlier, you said you knew other witches," I said when we hit a lull in the conversation.

"I meet all kinds of people in my line of work," Kurt said. "You're only the second I've met, though."

"And the first?"

"She was a client of mine." He turned into the massive casino parking lot. "Apparently, even witches have cheating spouses."

The casino was an explosion of lights and sounds and smells. Even the smallest win on the slot machines seemed to be met with chimes and music and cheers. We walked through a section where people openly smoked as they gambled. The health-nut inside me wanted to pluck every cigarette from their mouths and lecture them on the dangers of smoking. But I wasn't here to lecture anyone, I was here to have fun.

"It's very overwhelming," I said over the sound.

"Have you never been gambling before?"

I shook my head. His face widened in a smile.

"What are we waiting for?" he said. "Let's get going. Do you want to start with slots or with a table?"

"The slots look fun."

He wrapped an arm around my shoulders and pulled me in to whisper, "Walk around and only sit at the one that calls out to you. Wait for the feeling to strike, then go for it."

He stood back up and I laughed. He smiled at me and gave me a wink.

We walked around looking at the different machines, waiting for the feeling.

The feeling struck him first, and he stopped at a machine that had farm animals and aliens. "Keep going. I'll come find you."

I kept walking, trying to decide which machine was calling me. Finally, I saw one with the moon and a figure of a woman doing yoga on it. Perfect.

I slipped a ten-dollar bill into the slot and pushed the button.

Lights and sounds went off as the screen changed, lining up a bunch of yoga pose cards.

My ten dollars went up to nineteen. Instantly, I knew why people got addicted to gambling.

I pushed the button again, and the screen flashed into a big moon rising over a pond with the words Special Feature.

Without pushing anything, I watched as my money doubled and quadrupled.

A couple of people around me glanced over to see what my machine was doing. I smiled and kept watching.

Once the feature was over, I'd won enough to pay my utilities for a year.

I'd go one more time.

I bet the highest and pushed the button.

As the cards flashed on the screen, my chest was tight. If I won, I'd need to stop. If my magic was causing me to win, it would feel a lot like cheating. And I couldn't guarantee it wasn't.

Sure enough, the screen went ballistic, and the word jackpot appeared.

The number at the bottom that showed my winnings spun faster than I could read.

A crowd was gathering around behind me. "She won the jackpot," one woman said to another. "And she only played three times."

"Do you think she was cheating?" the other woman asked.

"How do you cheat a slot machine?" a man asked.

I pushed the print button to print out the ticket that declared I'd just become quite a bit richer. I shoved it into my satchel and pushed my way through the crowd.

"What's going on over there?" Kurt asked when I got back to his machine. He wasn't doing too shabby either.

"Someone won big," I said. "How are you doing?" I leaned on his machine just as he pushed the button, and the machine started going off with a Special Feature.

"Better now," he said.

A few of the people who had been crowding around me glanced over when they heard Kurt's machine go off.

"I'm going to find another machine," I said.

He just nodded as his winnings increased like mine had.

That settled it. My magic had cheated.

As I meandered around, careful not to touch any machines in passing, I considered my options. I could give the money back to the casino, but if they thought I won it cheating, they'd probably have me charged with a crime.

The slip was heavy in my bag. I'd have to cash it out, but I didn't want to do that in front of Kurt. So I headed to a window and slid it across the counter.

The woman who took it from me didn't react. She probably saw bigger sums every day. I'd heard stories of people winning big at casinos—Clancy being one of them.

As the woman in the window got a supervisor to watch her count my winnings, I glanced around at the people at the machines and card tables. Most of them looked so serious. I could hand the money out to them. Or go touch machines of the people who looked the saddest.

But my train of thought derailed when I saw a familiar face.

Weston sat at a card table with a large stack of chips in front of him.

I'd never played the game he was playing, but something made me want to join.

Maybe my magic was getting greedy. Or maybe it was giving me a nudge regarding Clancy's case.

"Ma'am?" the woman in the window said.

"Huh?"

"Would you like an escort to your car?"

I glanced at the stacks of bills she had in front of her, then down at my satchel. It would be tight, but it would fit.

"No, I'm okay," I said. "But thank you."

I made quick work of it, shoving the bills inside.

Weston looked like he'd just won another hand, and a couple of the people stood up from the table, taking their remaining chips.

The dealer was preoccupied with shuffling the cards. This was my opportunity.

"Hey," I said, walking up to the table.

Weston looked up at me. "Ellie, hi."

"We missed you in class today." Next to him was a long wooden cane.

"I didn't think there was much of a point learning the

tango when the only person I wanted to tango with was a murderer."

The dealer glanced up with a horrified look on her face, but Weston ignored her.

"You seem pretty certain she did it."

"Aren't you the one who found her covered in blood?"

I sighed. Of course, he'd heard about the incident in the barn. There were no secrets in Cliff Haven. At least not ones that lasted long.

"She swears it was her own blood. They're testing it now."

"Did you know she was leaving him for me? She left a note and everything."

It struck me funny that he knew about the note. But she had probably told him in the message she left from the jail.

"Why don't you seem happy about that?" I asked. "I thought you really liked her. I thought that's why you came to tango class."

He sighed. "It is. It was. I do like her. I love her."

"But you're pretty quick to accuse her of murder."

"If she didn't do it, why is she still in jail? I was released, and you found me covered in blood with a knife in my hand standing over the body."

Now everyone at the table was listening to our conversation.

"They're waiting for lab results," I said. "If what she said is true, she's been through quite the ordeal. She thought someone was after her, so she ran. Someone stole her car, and she fell down a cliff."

"Sounds pretty far-fetched," he said. "Though I've

never known Renée to lie. She was—is—a good woman. How she ended up with Clancy is beyond me. He was the worst of the worst."

"I'm sorry," one of the men next to me said. "I don't mean to pry into your conversation, but are you talking about Clancy Wright?"

"Yes," I said, spinning around to face him. "Did you know him?"

"Know him?" The man laughed. He had a gap between his front two teeth, which he filled with the end of a cigarette and spoke with it wedged in there. "Everyone knew Clancy Wright."

"Why is that?" I asked, trying not to breathe in the smoke swirling around my head.

"Did you say he's dead?" another man interrupted.

"He is," I said.

"Like confirmed dead?" the man with the cigarette asked.

"I fell on top of him," Weston said. "He was cold as ice."

"Who's in?" the dealer asked.

The two men who had asked about Clancy being dead both stood. "Not anymore," the one without the cigarette said. "Thanks for the info." He handed me a chip.

The other one put his cigarette out in one of the ashtrays on the table. "I'm going to take my wife out for a nice meal."

I turned back to Weston. "What was that all about?"

"I told you Clancy wasn't a good guy," he said. "He probably had dirt on those guys."

"Blackmail?"

"How do you think he made all that money?" Weston shook his head. "Certainly, not gambling."

I looked at the dealer for confirmation, but she said nothing.

If Clancy was blackmailing people, there could have been a whole other reason he ended up dead. And it certainly explained his house being in the state it was in. Whatever he had on whoever he had it on was probably trying to destroy the evidence.

"Am I dealing either of you in?" the dealer asked again.

"No thanks," I said.

"Nope," Weston said. He grabbed his cane and stood.

"Since when do you need a cane?"

"On and off since I was in my sixties," he said.

I glanced down at the innocent-looking walking stick and considered whether it could be the murder weapon. I hadn't seen Weston with a cane the night we found him on top of Clancy, but that didn't mean he didn't stash one somewhere.

"I saw you at the gas station earlier," I said. "You were filling a gas can?"

"Thankfully, my attorney hadn't left town," he said. "I didn't realize my truck was out of gas when I went to Renée's the other night."

This struck another nerve. If his truck had run out of gas, there was no telling how long he'd been there. It might have only died right before I fell on it.

"There you are," Kurt said, coming up next to us. "I've been looking all over for you."

"Who's this?" Weston asked.

"This is Kurt," I said. "He came to class tonight."

Kurt and Weston stood staring at each other for longer than seemed necessary.

"I don't mean to cut the night short," Kurt finally said to me, "but I just got a call from a VIP client who needs me immediately."

I'd already had my fair share of gambling.

"Why don't I take her home," Weston said. "Then you can go wherever you need to go straight away."

Kurt narrowed his eyes. "I'm perfectly okay taking her home."

"You said yourself your VIP client needs you immediately."

"They know I'm on a date and that I'll be there when I can get there."

When Kurt looked at me, Weston shook his head as if trying to warn me about Kurt.

"Why don't we let Ellie decide who she wants to take her home," Kurt said.

Neither of these men made my hair spark with danger. Even with several things pointing toward Weston being Clancy's killer.

"Kurt can take me home," I said. "Unless it would be easier if I went with Weston?"

Kurt looked at his watch. "No, it'll be just fine. But let's get a move on."

We started toward the door, but Weston grabbed my arm. "Be on your guard with that one."

"I will," I said.

Kurt looked back and glared at Weston again. Weston let go of my arm, and I followed Kurt out the door.

"What was that about?" I asked Kurt when we were outside. I almost had to jog to keep up with his pace.

"You shouldn't be alone with that man," Kurt said.

"Why not?"

We got into the car, and he started backing out of the parking spot before I had my seat belt on.

"He's dangerous," Kurt said. "That's all I can say."

"You know, I've had a lot of fun with you. I think you're a great guy. But if you keep pulling the confidentiality card—especially in regards to my safety—we can't hang out anymore."

He glanced over at me with an amused grin on his face. "Is that so?"

"Yep." I couldn't help but smile back at him. "So spill."

"I can't tell you how I know, but that man should be behind bars."

"For what?" I asked. "Because he was behind bars not so long ago for murder."

"Maybe he should have stayed there."

"Are you telling me you know something about the murder case?"

He shook his head. "I'm telling you it wouldn't surprise me in the slightest that he was a murderer."

"Because . . ."

"I wish I could tell you," Kurt said. "But I can't."

I shrugged and looked out the window. If he couldn't tell me, then that was it. We were done. Not that we had actually really started. Spending time at different slot machines in the same casino didn't exactly constitute as my dream date.

"How'd you end up doing on the slots?" he asked when we were only a few minutes from my house.

"I did okay," I said. "You?"

"Lost it all," he said. "I thought for a minute there I was going to be a big winner. If only I had stopped after I hit that feature."

He pulled into the driveway and put the car in park.

"I had a really nice time with you," he said. "I understand if you're mad at me and never want to see me again, but I'd like to see you when I get back to town."

I turned to face him. "You're leaving town?"

He nodded. "This client I have to visit isn't in Cliff Haven. But hopefully, I'll be back by Saturday's dance lesson." He grabbed my hand in his. "That is, if I'm still invited."

I couldn't help it. He was so sweet. "I guess you're still invited."

He squeezed my hand, then leaned forward as if he wanted to kiss me.

I leaned in, but something caught my eye in the back seat.

As his lips landed on my cheek, my gaze landed on a photograph peeking out from beneath a box. In the photo, plain as day, were Renée and Clancy, and written in black marker under Clancy's face were two words—Baby Bear.

A chill ran down my spine.

Baby Bear was Clancy.

Clancy was dead.

Kurt drove a white car.

"Wow, I didn't know a kiss on the cheek could have that effect." Kurt pulled back and pointed at my hair.

I had no doubt it was bright red.

I smiled as genuinely as I could. "Thanks for the date."

"We'll do it again," he said. "If you'll let me."

"Sure thing," I said, getting out of his car as calmly as I could.

I needed to call Jake.

He needed to catch Kurt before Kurt could hurt anyone else.

It took everything in me not to run to my front door and lock myself inside.

Instead, I turned and waved as he backed out so I could see which direction he was going.

The second he was out of sight, I ran up my stairs and started digging my house keys out of my satchel. They were buried under all the money.

I finally found them and was about to put the key in the door when a voice came from the shadow to my right.

"Did you have a nice time tonight?"

I nearly screamed, but when I saw Xander sitting on my porch swing, I stopped myself.

"What are you doing here?" I asked.

"Waiting for you."

"Well, I need to call Jake," I said, opening the door and walking inside. "Get in here and warm up. Where did you park?"

"Back by the barn." He followed me inside.

I tried to find my phone in my satchel, but the money was completely in the way. I started unloading it onto the kitchen counter.

"Whoa, did you rob a bank?"

"I'll tell you all about it after I find my—aha." I held my phone up triumphantly, then dialed Jake's number.

"Hello?" Jake said.

"Jake, I know who killed Clancy, and he's getting away," I said.

"Slow down," Jake said. "What do you mean he's getting away?"

"It was Kurt, the P.I. who was at the dance class tonight."

"Kurt never mentioned he was a P.I."

"He doesn't like to tell people things," I said. "Probably because he's a murderer. Seriously, you need to get a car heading east away from my house before he turns, and we don't know where he went."

"What does the car look like?"

I gave him the description of the rental car. Jake called out on his radio for the nearest car to pull Kurt over under suspicion of murder.

"Can you tell me what's going on now?" Jake asked.

Xander was staring at me as I paced around the kitchen.

"I went out with Kurt tonight. To the casino up north. We got into an accident on the way there in his white car. The same color car I saw pulling out onto the highway from Clancy and Renée's house the night we found Clancy dead."

Xander's eyes lit up in recognition.

"I heard about the accident, but they said everyone was okay."

"We were," I said. "So he got a rental car delivered, and we still went to the casino. I saw Weston there. He had a cane, which I thought meant he might have killed Clancy, but Kurt had a bat in the back of his car so it could have been either of them."

I took a breath.

"Let me back up," I said. "When I first met Kurt, he asked me whether I knew anyone who went by the name of Baby Bear. And tonight, I saw a picture in the back of his car—his rental car—after we switched everything over. The picture was of Renée and Clancy, and under Clancy's head was the name Baby Bear written in permanent marker."

"You think Kurt killed Clancy as part of his business?" Jake asked.

"Possibly," I said. "Or he was looking through the house and Clancy came home and one thing led to another."

"Anything else?"

"Weston didn't want me to go home with Kurt," I said. "Maybe he saw Kurt that night. Maybe he saw him kill Clancy, and that's why he didn't want me to go with him."

I was such an idiot. I should have listened to Weston's warning. I could have been next.

In the background, I heard an officer call over the radio. "We found him."

"They found Kurt?" I asked.

"Sounds like it," Jake said.

"He's evading," the officer said.

"He's what?" I asked.

"He's running," Jake said. "But they'll get him."

"What if they don't?" I asked. "He'll know I said something."

"Call Xander and see if he'll stay with you," Jake said. "And keep the doors locked."

"Xander's already here," I said.

"Good," Jake said. "I'll let you know what we find."

We disconnected, and Xander tilted his head to the side. "Exciting night, then?"

I couldn't help the tears that started flowing down my cheeks.

Xander gathered me up in his arms. "Shh, it's okay." He stroked my hair, smoothing down the red frizz. "They'll get him."

I tried to gather my emotions, but I was all over the place—Xander hugging me, Kurt being a murderer, Weston's warning. I wouldn't have been surprised if my hair resembled a disco ball at the moment.

"Why were you waiting for me?" I asked, remembering him sitting on my porch in the freezing cold.

"It doesn't matter right now," Xander said.

I pulled back and looked up into his eyes. "Please tell me."

He took a step back and shoved his hands in his pockets. "I was going to talk to you about trying to find your mom."

"Right," I said. He hadn't seemed too happy in the barn when he realized why the mural had changed so drastically. "Why were you so upset about that?"

"Upset?" Xander asked. "It didn't upset me you were trying to find your mom. It upset me you practically drained all your magic and looked completely exhausted."

That made sense. "I just need to keep exercising it. And then maybe I'll be able to find her."

"Let's focus on one mystery at a time, okay?" Xander smiled. "Also, what is it with you and dating terrible men?"

I gaped at him. "What do you mean? This is the first truly terrible one I've dated."

"You might have dated that other one—the one who was living here before you."

Ugh. He was right. I might have. Until he killed a bunch of people. "He was dating someone."

Xander shrugged.

"And I'm not dating Kurt," I said. "We went on a date. That's it. And at least he accepted my hair for what it was. He's the first guy who didn't seem to care."

"He probably thought your magic could scrub his murderous record."

"What about you?"

"What about me?" Xander leaned back against the counter.

"You and Laura looked pretty flirty tonight," I said. "It's funny because she always claims to hate magic."

"She hates women who are prettier than her—magical or not," Xander said. "But what woman doesn't?"

"Um, me," I said. "I'm friends with lots of women who are prettier than me."

"That's debatable," he said.

I could feel my hair changing at his compliment. I sucked in a breath and changed my thoughts back to the night I'd had.

"But Laura's nice," he said. "She's polite and sweet and a good dancer."

Penelope oinked beside me, nearly making me jump. She was warning me that my hair was changing, but I thought she was still sleeping. I reached down and scooped her up. "I went out with a murderer tonight."

She tilted her head, her floppy ears perking up, then she looked at Xander.

"Don't look at me," he said. "If she would have asked, I would have told her something was off about that guy."

"Oh sure," I said, putting Penelope back on the floor. "You knew he was a murderer?"

"Not a murderer, per se." Xander pushed off from the counter. "I just didn't see you with him, that's all."

"If you don't see me with him, who do you see me with?"

Xander rubbed the stubble on his chin. "That's tough." He walked through the kitchen slowly. "Someone who accepts you for who you are, obviously."

"Obviously," I said with a smile.

"Who doesn't freak out at the slightest change in your hair."

I almost said, duh, but held it in.

"Someone who will let you be yourself, even if that means holding back when they know you're about to make a mistake."

"Not that I make any mistakes," I said.

"Of course not." He glanced over his shoulder at me and grinned. "But also someone who will call you out when you need it."

"That's a pretty vague description."

Penelope peeked around the island, watching what Xander was doing.

"You want more detail?"

"It wouldn't hurt."

"Fine." Xander waved a hand in the air. "Someone tall and strong. With great hair." He ran a hand through his hair.

"Someone magical?" I asked.

He shrugged. "Wouldn't hurt. It's hard to find a non-magical person to accept our magic. Trust me. I've tried."

I didn't doubt it.

So had I.

"But they exist. Even ones who haven't murdered anyone."

I laughed. "Can you believe I went out with a murderer?"

As if on cue, my phone rang.

"Is it Jake?" Xander asked.

I couldn't say the words. I just shook my head no.

"Who is it—oh," he said, taking a glance at the screen. "Why do you think he's calling?"

"Maybe to yell at me for calling the police on him," I said. "To threaten me."

Dread crept up my neck, into my scalp.

I picked up the phone.

"You're not going to answer it, are you?"

I shouldn't have. But I had to. I had to know why he was calling.

"Hello?" I said, my voice shaky.

"Hey, Ellie." Kurt sounded perfectly calm. "Sorry if I woke you."

"I wasn't asleep."

"That's a relief."

"What's up?"

"I wanted to let you know I probably wouldn't make it back for class on Saturday. But I didn't want you to think I didn't have fun tonight."

"Uh—okay."

Xander gave me a questioning look.

"Is there any reason you might not make it?" I asked.

"There's this client—not the one who called me tonight, another one—who has a pressing matter. I'm hopeful it won't take longer than a week or so to figure out, but it might."

"Thanks for letting me know."

"Definitely," he said a smile in his voice. "I hope you'll still be available when I come back. But I understand if you're not. I don't want you putting your life on hold for me."

There was approximately zero chance I'd be available to date him. Not now. "Good luck with your client."

He seemed a bit bummed I hadn't told him I'd wait for him, but I didn't want to lie. "Thanks. I'll see you later."

"Bye."

I hung up and put my phone back on the counter.

"So?" Xander asked.

"He wanted to let me know he'll be out of town longer than he thought, but he still wants to take me out when he comes back."

"Did he say anything about the police following him?"

I shook my head. "I didn't hear any sirens in the background either. He sounded perfectly content."

My phone rang again. This time Jake's face appeared on the screen.

"Hello?" I said, knowing what he was going to tell me.

"They lost him," Jake said. "He took a back road and disappeared."

"He just called me."

"And said what?"

"That he'll be out of town longer than he expected, but he still wants to take me out on a date."

"That doesn't sound like something a murderer would say minutes after he evaded a police chase," Jake said. "Are you absolutely certain of what you saw in his back seat?"

"I'm certain," I said, thinking back to the items I'd seen. "He had a bat, balls, files, what looked like a smashed phone, some fishing gear, and the photos. Plus, why else would he have run from the police?"

"I agree with your point. Is Xander still there?"

"Yeah," I said. "Why? Do you think I'm in danger?"

"No," Jake said. "From what we could tell, Kurt was truly heading out of town as quickly as possible. He'd be an idiot to come back when he knows the entire police force is looking for him."

"Then why did you want to know if Xander was still here?"

"I need to talk to him, if you don't mind."

I handed Xander the phone. "Jake wants to talk to you."

Xander took it and listened to what Jake said with a few acknowledging words, then hung up. "He said to tell you bye."

"What else did he say?" I asked.

"He wanted to tell me about his date with Georgia."

"Why?" That was not at all what I expected.

"Because I set them up."

"You set them up and didn't tell me?"

"Why would I tell you? Do you have a thing for Jake?"

"Ew," I said. "No."

"That's good. He's old enough to be your father."

"But he's not my father."

"I know," Xander said. "But still."

I sighed. "I guess I didn't realize you were close like that."

"We're not really, but since Georgia's my cousin—"

"Wait," I said, holding up a hand. "Georgia is your cousin? Does that mean she's a witch?"

"I thought you knew." He shrugged. "Apparently, Jake has a thing for witches."

It was my turn to pace the kitchen. But where Xander had paced slowly and methodically, I was practically speed stomping. "Is there a way to know when someone is a witch or warlock?"

"You use your magic," Xander said. He and Penelope both watched as I walked back and forth.

"How?" I asked, stopping in front of him. "How do I use my magic to tell if someone else has magic? Do I have to do it on every single person I meet? Why can't it just be obvious?"

Xander grabbed me by the shoulders. "El, it's okay."

I sucked in a breath.

"You've had a big night. Maybe we should talk about this in the morning."

"How do I know? How do I use my magic like that?"

"Eventually, it's just second nature," he said. "Eventually, you'll just see someone and know. You'll sense it."

I shrugged his hands off. "I'm tired. I think I'll go to bed." I wasn't actually that tired, but I was tired of him and his vague answers to my magical questions.

"Hold on," Xander said.

"Yeah?" Hope rose in my chest. Was he going to tell me more about my magic?

"Where did you get all that money?" He pointed to the money on the island that I'd completely forgotten about.

"The casino," I said. "Apparently, magic helps with gambling. I didn't mean to, but the machines just went crazier every time I played."

Xander burst out laughing.

"What?" I asked. "It's probably against some magical law, isn't it? I can return the money. I don't want it, anyway."

"It's not against magical law—wait—you're saying you really won this at the casino? Using your magic?"

"I didn't mean to use my magic," I said. "It just sort of happened. I only pushed the button three times."

Xander glanced at the money, then back at me. "You didn't win that with your magic. That's not how magic works."

"Then why did Kurt's machine start winning the moment I touched it?"

"Lady luck?" Xander said. "You won that money fair and square."

With one hundred percent certainty, I knew my magic had something to do with those winnings, but I wasn't in the mood to debate it with him. "Okay."

Xander walked toward the back door. "I'll see you later."

"See ya," I said. I felt like a child who just realized maybe adults didn't have all the answers. Xander obviously didn't know all the ins and outs of magic. Or at least my magic.

I put the money in one of the lower cabinets behind a bunch of appliances, then rushed up the stairs to my room and slid open the bookcase, revealing the passageway to the attic. Penelope hurried up the staircase behind me and sat at my feet when I plopped down in the chair.

I opened Esme's journal, flipping through page after page, looking for answers. But nothing new stood out to me.

I groaned in frustration. "I need to know how to use my magic."

The pages fell limp in my lap, almost as if they were as worn out as I was.

I turned to the back of the journal and started writing, letting the words flow out of me. I documented my frustrations and how sometimes I felt like my magic might burst out of me if I didn't figure out how to use it properly. I wrote about Xander and Kurt and the case.

And by the time I'd written everything down, I felt

somewhat better. Like I always did after writing in Esme's journal.

"Should we go to bed?" I asked Penelope, who was already asleep at my feet.

She looked up at me, then looked at the journal and oinked quietly.

"I already wrote in it," I said.

She oinked again.

There wasn't anything left to write about.

But I was learning not to dismiss Penelope when she tried to communicate something to me.

I picked the pen back up and turned the pages, when I saw a page I hadn't seen before translated so I could read it.

My heart started beating harder in my chest as I read one single line.

Find the study, my darling granddaughter. Find the study.

My chest filled with excitement. Penelope, noticing the change in my mood and hair, spun in a circle.

"We have to find the study."

We started upstairs and worked our way down. Every last bedroom. Every last nook and cranny. We searched for hours but found no sign of a study. If not for the exhaustion creeping up on me, I would have kept going.

Instead, Penelope and I went to bed with more questions than answers.

The ladies were all on time for their morning class, gathering in the barn with hot mugs of coffee in their hands.

This morning, in addition to the usual Katie, Amy, Fran, Nancy, and Bonnie, Bex and Deb joined us too.

"I hear they released Renée early this morning," Nancy said to Deb as they haphazardly stretched while drinking coffee.

"You heard correctly," Deb said.

"Wait," I said. "Does that mean she's been cleared?"

"Yep," Deb said. "Not enough evidence to hold her. And without you pressing actual charges—against my advice—there was no way to keep her in jail."

I didn't bring up the fact that we also had it on good authority that she definitely wasn't the one who had killed Clancy.

"So where'd she go?" Nancy asked.

"She drove home," Deb said. "A few days ago, we found her stolen car. We think some teenagers took it for a joyride then left it at the square."

"I'm glad you found her car," I said. "She was probably itching to get home and get her house back in order."

Deb nodded. "We're hopeful she'll be able to find what we couldn't—either her phone or Clancy's."

"What time was she released?" I asked.

"I got off about an hour ago," Deb said. "So probably around then."

"Maybe I'll stop over there after class," I said.

"She'd probably like that," Deb said. "And maybe she'd be willing to give you any information."

She might, but I still wasn't sure what I would do with any information she gave me but didn't want me to give to the police. "I'll see what I can do."

Deb nodded and went back to talking to Bex.

I meandered over to Katie and the others. "Hey, ladies," I said. "I have a quick question before we start."

"What is it, sweetheart?" Nancy said.

"Do you know where Esme's study might be in the house?" I asked.

They looked at each other, then each of them shook their heads. I couldn't help but feel disappointed.

"But sometimes she seemed to appear out of nowhere," Katie said. "Have you checked the basement?"

"Basement?" I asked. "I didn't know there was a basement."

"Silly goose," Nancy said. "There are basement windows all around your foundation."

"Do you know how to access the basement?" I asked.

"Probably through what looks like a closet," Fran said. "Or maybe a hatch in the floor."

"Or an outside access," Amy said.

If it was outside, there was no way I would get to it before spring. "Thanks," I said. "We should probably get started."

The class went by so slowly, I nearly called it quits early. I desperately wanted to get over to Renée's house to see how she was doing.

As we finished up, Katie walked outside. "Feels like it might be warmer today."

"We could sure use more of those," Amy said.

"Before we know it, we'll be complaining it's too hot," Fran said. "Never satisfied."

They all laughed.

I had yet to live an Iowa summer, but I'd heard they could be brutal with the heat and humidity.

"I'll see you ladies tomorrow," I said.

"Let me know if you hear anything from Renée," Deb whispered. "Maybe she can shed some light on what Baby Bear meant and whether Kurt had motive to kill her husband."

"I'll see what I can do."

22

B y the time I got to Renée and Clancy's house, the sun was up and was actually melting some of the snow. Though it wouldn't be enough to get rid of all the snow and ice, it was nice to have warmer weather.

I knocked on the door and heard footsteps.

Jasmine opened the door and invited me inside.

"Renée will be with you in a moment," she said and started toward the kitchen.

"How was your vacation?"

"It was lovely," she said.

"And you were gone this entire time?"

"I don't believe that's any of your business," she said. "But if you must know, the police already questioned me about my whereabouts when the crime occurred. I only returned last night."

"Ellie, you're here," Renée said, coming down the stairs.

"I wanted to check on you to see how you're doing."

"I'm doing okay." She pointed to the mess still around her. "Jasmine and I are slowly picking up the pieces."

"Have you found either your or Clancy's phones?" I asked.

She motioned for me to follow her, then whispered, "You're not going to believe what else I found."

We walked into what I figured was Clancy's destroyed office. Though some of the mess was organized into piles.

"Have you heard from Weston?" I asked. After our discussion at the casino, I figured he'd be one of the first people to contact her when she got out of jail. Though maybe he didn't know she was out yet.

"I don't think he ever really wanted to be with me. If he had, don't you think he would have bailed me out of jail or at least come to visit?"

"Didn't they tell you?"

"Tell me what?"

"Weston was in jail too."

Her eyes widened. "Why? Please tell me he didn't kill Clancy. That's not what I meant. Oh goodness, he did, didn't he? This is all my fault."

"What do you mean?"

"I might have mentioned to Weston that the only way we could be together is if Clancy died." She plopped down in the desk chair. "I didn't mean for Weston to kill Clancy."

"I don't think he did," I said, though it was still possible with the cane and his presence at the crime scene. Not to mention the gas to fill his empty tank. That could have meant that he was there longer than I originally thought.

"Why was Weston in jail, then?" Renée asked.

"When Xander and I came here to check on you after dance class, we found Weston standing over Clancy's body holding a knife. He fell on top of Clancy and seemed to get Clancy's blood on him." My brain tried to process this. Had he gotten blood on him because he'd fallen on him and in the puddle of blood, or because he'd killed Clancy, after all?

"Is he still in jail?" she asked.

"They released him."

"Then they must think he's innocent." Her face brightened slightly. "Maybe I should call him." She pulled her phone out of the pocket of her jeans.

"Did you check your phone to see if there was anything suspicious about the cameras or the security system?"

She shook her head. "I forgot about it."

"Can we look now?"

She handed me the phone. "You remember the passcode?"

I typed in one-two-three-four, and the phone opened to a screen of small icons with a picture of what I assumed was Argentina in the background.

"That's the app." She pointed to one of the blue apps on the screen. I tapped it and started through the thousands of notifications.

I thought back to before Clancy was killed. Every day there were hundreds of notifications from the deck door. When I clicked on each video, almost all of them showed the same thing—an empty deck with no movement. Every once in a while, a bird would land on the rail, or a gust of wind would move the camera. But for the most part, nothing explained why the notification kept going off.

"The system's faulty," she said. "It's not going to help, anyway."

I kept going.

I saw the comings and goings of Renée, Clancy, and Jasmine. A couple of times, I was either pulling in or out of the driveway in Mona.

Then I saw the last class I had with Renée. I arrived, Jasmine left, and shortly after I left, Renée left in her car.

After that, the only person to come and go in the driveway was Clancy.

I scrolled through to get to the date of Clancy's death.

Every once in a while I checked the deck notifications to find more false alarms.

I slowed to a stop the night before I found Clancy. He arrived home around six o'clock, stumbling as though he might have been intoxicated.

"He looks drunk," Renée said.

The notifications slowed through the night and then picked up again in the morning on the deck.

"The false alarms are so random," I said. "But they mostly seem to be during the day. Maybe the sun glares off something causing it."

Renée looked down at her nails as if this was all boring her.

I clicked on the last notification before a long stretch without any. The video showed a hand reaching up and covering the camera with something. Everything went dark.

Renée gasped. "What was that?"

"It looks like someone covered the camera."

I scrolled to the next video, time-stamped three hours later. Whatever had been covering the camera was removed, revealing a dark deck and a police officer looking up into the lens.

I went back to the video where the camera had been covered and slowed it down.

"Does anything look familiar to you about this?" I held it so Renée could see it, too.

We watched it several times over and over again, but there wasn't much to see.

"Whoever did it either would have had to have a ladder or been relatively tall," Renée said.

Both Kurt and Weston were easily six-foot-tall, meaning either of them could have done it.

"Hold on," I said. "Is that a tattoo?" I tried to zoom in on the video, but it got all grainy. I zoomed back out. "See there? On the wrist?"

Renée brought the phone close to her face, then held it at arm's length, then brought it close again. "I can't tell."

I looked again. "It sure looks like a tattoo. Does Weston have a tattoo on his wrist?"

"No idea," she said. "It's not like we were physically intimate."

If only I'd looked at Kurt's arms more closely.

The rest of the notifications were of the police coming and going. I handed her back her phone, frustration encompassing me.

"Ready to see what I found now?" Renée wiggled her eyebrows at me.

I smiled. "Definitely."

23

Renée handed me a bunch of photos. I leafed through them. "What am I looking at?"

"Look closer," she said, an eager smile on her face.

The photos seemed to be of several men embracing the same woman. Most of them were grainy and had objects blocking parts of the photos.

"I don't get it," I said. "These look like some creep was spying on people hooking up."

"I think that creep was Clancy," she said. "Turn them over."

I turned one of them over to find a phone number, days and times, and dates next to dollar amounts.

When I flipped it back over, I realized the man looked familiar. His face was in plain view as he held the much younger woman in his arms.

I looked at it more closely.

Where had I seen him before?

Then it dawned on me. I'd seen him at the casino. He

had been at the table with Weston. He was the one who asked if Clancy was confirmed dead.

"Renée," I said. "Is this what I think it is?"

But she wasn't listening. Something had distracted her.

As I scanned through the backs of a few more photos, some of the dollar figures were small amounts, but most were in the thousands of dollars.

"I can't believe it." Renée stood, holding what looked like a necklace in her hand. "I thought he might have gotten rid of it." Tears welled up in her eyes as she cradled the charm in her palm. She lowered it to show me. It was the paw print she typically wore around her neck.

"Baby Bear," I said, realization washing over me.

Her head shot up. "What did you say?"

"You called him Baby Bear, didn't you?"

"How did you know that?" Renée asked, fastening the necklace around her neck.

"I think we need to take this to the police," I said. "I think these photos are the reason Clancy was murdered."

"I'm sorry, Ellie," she said. "I can't do that. Not yet."

"Why not?" I was shocked.

"Because there's someone I need to talk to before I do."

"But you could be in danger," I said. "If they know you have this information, they could come after you too."

"You're my friend," she said. "But I need you to trust me on this. I'll call the police just as soon as I can. Right now, though, I need you to leave."

I thought maybe she was joking. Until she took the photos out of my hand and pointed toward the door.

The moment I got to Mona, I called Jake.

"Hello?"

"Jake, it's Ellie," I said. "There's something you need to know."

I told him about what Renée and I had found, and he said he'd have someone head to Renée's house right away.

Unfortunately, by the time I was walking through my front door, he called back.

"She let us in, but we found nothing. She said you must have been mistaken."

I groaned in frustration.

"I know, kiddo, but we'll figure it out. Now that we know Clancy might have been blackmailing people, we have a whole new direction to take the investigation."

When we hung up, I sat on the stairs, scratching Penelope behind the ears. Clancy's case was out of my hands. The feeling was like a rock had settled in the pit of my stomach. Frustration was quickly becoming one of my body's go-to emotions, and I didn't like it.

"Penelope, I need to do something," I said. "I need a breakthrough."

She oinked and took off down the hall toward the kitchen. I laughed. Food was almost always her go-to when emotions were too much to handle.

"I'm not hungry," I yelled after her, but she just oinked back at me as if telling me to follow her.

I sighed. Sometimes Penelope was like my best friend, others she was like a toddler.

"What is it?" I expected her to be standing by the

fridge or maybe the pantry door waiting for me to make some popcorn with peanut butter, but instead, she was peeking around the back side of the island. The side furthest from the kitchen entrance.

"What are you doing over there?"

She oinked again.

When I turned the corner, I saw it. It was brief, but it was there.

A speck of magic.

My pulse quickened. Tingles wound their way up my neck to my scalp. Out of the corner of my eye, I saw my hair tightening into spiral curls.

I focused on the place I'd seen the magic before it disappeared.

A glimmer peeked out again.

Penelope let out an excited squeal.

I reached down to where the island met the floor— where the magic seemed to be seeping out.

The moment my finger touched the sparkle, it felt like a string of electricity slipped through the tip of my finger, up my arm, and into my hair. The spirals loosened to waves as I focused on the magic.

In one fluid motion, the island swiveled to the left, revealing a hole in the floor. I stepped back and watched as a swirl of magical specks floated up from the staircase, descending into the floor. A hint of lilac wafted up, tickling my nose.

Without a word, I lifted Penelope into my arms and practically floated down the staircase.

Most farmhouse basements were musty and damp, but

the air only seemed to become clearer and purer as I reached the bottom step.

Darkness hid what seemed to be a rather large room, judging by the echoes of my footsteps. I focused on my magic, willing it to go forth into the room and brighten the walls.

For the first time, my magic did exactly as I wanted it to.

The walls—a sort of plaster—glowed, starting at the floor and moving to the ceiling. The farther I descended into the underground study, the more the room opened up into a magical oasis bathed in warm light.

Heavy wooden beams extended across the ceiling, which seemed much too high for how deep I'd ventured underground. The magic of the place hummed as I touched the surface of the polished wooden desks, the stone work tables, and shelf after shelf of thick leather-bound books.

There was so much to see. So much to read. It overwhelmed my senses.

Penelope wriggled in my arms so I'd put her down.

She nudged the back of my leg, pushing me toward a chair in front of one of the desks. This particular desk had a neat pile of scrolls stacked toward the wall and candles that had once been lit, their wax spilling down their sides onto the desk.

A single sheet of paper rested in the center of the desk as if patiently waiting for its time to be read.

I sat in the chair and lifted the sheet, another wave of lilac overcoming my senses.

You found it, just as I knew you would. I do hope I've left the study in a state you find manageable. It wasn't easy with prying eyes, but I snuck away as necessary to tidy up. I was thrilled to find that the family lineage wouldn't stop with Emily. It is my dying wish that you will find your way back to one another.

As you may have found by now, my sweet granddaughter, Cliff Haven is much less quiet than I described in my letter. It was one of my greatest pleasures helping the police solve so many cases. You may also have the knack for crime-solving. If so, I wish you well. Stay safe and vigilant. And tell Jake I say hi. I love you, Ellie.

Oh, and one more thing: you have powerful magic running through your veins, but sometimes things have to reveal themselves over time. Push, but don't push too hard.

I placed the piece of paper back on the desk and sat back in the chair where my grandmother had likely sat to write the letter to me. If I closed my eyes and focused, I could almost feel her arms wrapping around me in a hug.

Penelope let out a low oink next to me and nudged my hand.

I pulled her into my lap and kissed her wiggly snout.

"I wish I could have met her," I whispered.

Penelope nuzzled into me, letting me hug her as tight as I needed.

Unfortunately, our snuggles came to an abrupt end when my phone rang in the kitchen above us. It was strange, for being so far underground, I could hear the ring of my phone with almost perfect clarity.

"I should probably get that." Penelope and I hurried back up the stairs. When we were back in the kitchen, the island slid into place as if there was nothing beneath it.

"Hello?" I answered without even looking at who was calling.

"Ellie?" Renée's voice came through the phone. "I'm ready to talk to the police. Will you come over so we can talk to them together?"

"I'll be right there."

24

Within minutes, I was at Renée's door. She opened it before I could knock.

"Where's Jasmine?"

"She left when I confronted her."

"Confronted her about what?" I asked as I took off my shoes.

"I'll show you."

On their large dining table, she had all the pictures—the ones she told the police didn't exist—spread out.

"Look at these and tell me what's different." She handed me two pictures.

I took a glance. "This one was taken at night, and this one during the day?"

"Look closer." She looked like she might burst if I didn't figure it out quickly.

I glanced back and forth between the two photos.

Then I saw it.

"That's—"

"Jasmine!" Renée interrupted, practically jumping up and down. "They were working together. She was a trap. I wanted to give her a chance to explain herself. She was like a daughter to me. But when I asked her about the photos, she just stormed out. I think she killed Clancy."

"Why would she have killed Clancy?"

"To keep all the money for herself," Renée said. "It makes so much sense now. She pretended to have a vacation coming up, but she never actually went out of town. Then she snuck inside, demolished the house trying to find the photos, and when she couldn't find them, she killed Clancy."

It sounded possible, but something just wasn't adding up. "I can see how you've come to that conclusion. But hear me out."

She shoved her fists into her hips and gave me a skeptical look.

"Why would she come to work today after she killed Clancy? Heck, why would she work for you at all if she was making money working with Clancy on these gigs? Maybe she's a prostitute on the side and Clancy found out. But even if she knew Clancy had photos, she wouldn't need to cover up your camera, sneak into your house, and destroy it. She has a key, right? And full access to the house even when you aren't home."

Renée seemed baffled by this thought.

I glanced down at all the photographs. Clancy had to have been making a killing off all these men. Sure, they had a nice house and all, but it wasn't this nice.

The chime rang on the deck, and we both froze.

"Ellie," Renée whispered. "I didn't notice it until now, but that hasn't gone off a single time since I've been back."

I thought back to the app on her phone. The multiple alarms had stopped after Clancy died. The only ones afterward had been for the police coming and going.

The alarm went off again.

I took a step toward the sliding door.

"Don't," Renée said.

"Call the police," I said. "Tell them to get here as soon as possible."

I could hear Renée talking in whispers on the phone as I inched my way to the door.

The alarm went off again.

Someone was out there. I could see the top of their head as they stood on the other side of the deck.

I ducked down and tried to see what they were doing, and why they weren't actually coming onto the deck.

"The police are on their way," Renée whispered.

"Someone's out there," I said.

"We have lattice around underneath the deck," Renée said. "Maybe they've been hiding under there."

I doubted anyone would hide under her deck in this weather, but anything was possible.

"Can you see what they're doing?"

I took another step and crouched down, but my movement caught the person's eye.

A person I knew.

Kurt.

His eyes widened at the sight of me.

I rushed to the door and threw it open. "What are you doing?"

He didn't stick around to answer me. He took off running into the sunset like a track star, though his progress was slow through the deep snow.

I shouted his name and stepped out onto the deck, but my foot caught something. I toppled, face-down.

"Oh, my goodness," Renée said behind me. "Are you okay?"

"I tripped," I said.

"On what?"

I pushed up and noticed my hand was only inches from the bloody print on the deck. I wasn't the first one to trip out here.

"Do you see anything?" I asked. "A nail or maybe a loose board?"

Renée shook her head. "There's nothing there."

A knock at the front door took Renée's attention. "It's probably the police."

She walked away, and I stood. My foot had caught on something, but what?

I started back inside, dragging my feet along the boards, when I felt something stop my ankle.

It was an invisible barrier.

"Why are you here?" Renée's voice came from the front door. I couldn't see who she was talking to, but I would guess it wasn't the police.

"Who is it?" I glanced back over my shoulder to see the speck of Kurt still running away through the snowy field.

"Weston," Renée called over her shoulder.

I stepped over the barrier and marched inside.

"What are you doing here?" I asked, coming to stand next to Renée.

"I wanted to check on Renée," he said to me, then turned to Renée. "When I heard you had been released, I came right over."

"Did you do it?" Renée asked. "Did you kill Clancy?"

Weston's eyes darkened. "You know I would do anything to be with you."

My scalp tingled. Was he really confessing right here and now?

"So you did kill him?" Renée looked like she might pass out.

"No," he said. "Killing your husband wouldn't allow us to be together. I'd be in jail."

Renée's knees went soft. I reached over and caught her before she fell to the ground.

Weston crouched down next to us and took Renée into his arms. "I'm so sorry Clancy died."

"How could someone murder him? I mean, I know he wasn't nice, and apparently he was blackmailing a lot of people, but still," Renée said.

"Maybe someone got tired of being blackmailed and found out who he was," Weston said, then looked at me. "Someone like that boyfriend of yours."

"Or one of his clients," I said.

I stood and went back to the sliding door.

I cursed myself for not going after Kurt. Not that I would have known what to do with him if I'd caught him. But I could have at least tried to use my magic. Though that might have backfired too, and I could have hurt him instead of simply detaining him.

"Good, you're here," Renée said behind me.

I turned to find Jake walking in. "I hear there's something you need to tell us."

I glanced over at the photos. "Before we talk about that," I said. "Kurt was just here. He took off running that way through the snowy field."

Jake got on his radio and called out a BOLO—be on the lookout—for Kurt.

I bent down to inspect where I'd tripped to find a piece of fishing line. "Check this out." I followed it to the side of the deck, right by where Kurt had been. "I tripped over this earlier. I think it's probably what caused that bloody handprint." I pulled on the line. "And the false alarms." Sure enough, the line moved, and a small lure popped up onto the deck.

"Interesting," Jake said. "It's tied all the way around."

"If I had to guess," I said. "Kurt found out that Clancy was Baby Bear at the request of one of his clients. He was going to break in and get the incriminating photos, but to do so, he'd have to desensitize Renée and Clancy to the door chime."

"So he set up a lure on a clear strand of fishing line

and would pull it repeatedly throughout the day to make the sensor go off," Jake said. "The camera isn't good enough quality to pick up the actual lure."

"Or the tattoo that I suspect is on Kurt's wrist," I said. "He put something over the camera about three hours before a police officer took it off the night Xander and I found Clancy."

"You think he came in here and trashed the house looking for the photos?" Jake looked out at the horizon. "And when Clancy tried to stop him, he killed him?"

"Possibly," I said. Maybe it was because I went on a date with him, or maybe it was because of intuition, but something didn't seem right with that scenario.

"You're not certain?"

I shook my head no.

A voice came over the radio. "We got him. Do you want us to take him to the station?"

Jake clicked the mic on his shoulder. "Bring him to me."

Everyone stopped and looked at Jake.

"We're going to settle this here and now," Jake said.

I paced the kitchen, my throat dry. "Renée, do you mind if I get some water?"

"Not at all," she said.

"Does anyone else want some?" I asked.

Everyone shook their heads.

I grabbed a glass from the cabinet and pressed it up to the ice dispenser. Ice shot out all over the floor, not a single cube making it into my cup. "Oh man, I'm sorry."

"That stupid ice machine," Renée said. "Jasmine was supposed to call someone about that."

I bent down to scoop up the ice cubes, then deposited them into the sink before carefully getting fresh ice and water.

The water did practically nothing to quench my thirst. I felt like I'd run a marathon without a single bit of hydration.

"Here he is," an officer came in with a handcuffed Kurt.

Jake walked up to him. "Did you kill Clancy Wright?"

"No," Kurt said. "He did."

He couldn't point, but I knew who he was referring to.

"Who are you speaking of?" Jake asked.

"Weston," Kurt said. "He was in the house when Clancy was murdered, and Ellie caught him covered in Clancy's blood."

"I didn't kill Clancy," Weston said. "You did. You ran when I caught you."

"Why didn't you tell us that?" Jake asked Weston.

"I was afraid he'd come after me. He saw my face." Weston looked genuinely terrified of Kurt. "I didn't want to be his next victim."

"You don't know what you're talking about, old man." Kurt's face was red, probably from running across the field only to be caught by the cops.

"Just tell us what happened," Jake said. "Why were you in the Wright's house that night?"

Kurt sighed. "I was hired to find out who was blackmailing one of my clients. The only name he had was Baby Bear. I followed Jasmine to Cliff Haven after one of their rendezvous."

Everyone seemed to be on the edges of their seats, listening to his story. Me included.

"She led me here," Kurt said. "Right to him."

"How did you know Clancy was Baby Bear?" Renée asked.

"There are bears on your mailbox," Kurt said. "And since this is a brand new house—and brand new mailbox —I figured the odds were pretty good. All I had to do was follow him a couple of times as he followed Jasmine to confirm he was the one I was looking for."

"So you rigged up a fishing line to make the sensors go off to desensitize Clancy and Renée," I said.

"That was one of my more brilliant plans," Kurt said. "I figured if I could get them to leave the door unlocked after checking to see what was on the deck, I could get in and find the photographs."

"And?"

"Clancy finally left it unlocked," Kurt said. "I think he was drunk. So I waited until it got dark and went inside. But I couldn't find the photos anywhere."

"Clancy could have had digital backups," Jake said.

"He was a geezer." Kurt shrugged. "There was no way he would have relied on technology."

Kurt had a point, especially since he literally kept notes on the back of each photograph.

"When you were searching, weren't you worried Clancy would find you?" I asked.

"At first, yes," Kurt said. "But the more noise I made, the more I figured he was either passed out or had left. Until I found him."

"What do you mean?" Renée asked.

"I tripped right over him," Kurt said. "I came into the kitchen, and there he was. My hand landed in something sticky and wet. When I stood up to examine it, I realized I wasn't alone."

Renée gasped and looked over at Weston.

"Oh sure," Weston said. "That's a likely story. You know I didn't kill him because you did. You just figured since I was there too, you could pin it on me."

Kurt shook his head. "You were holding a knife."

"Because the house was trashed," Weston said. "I figured someone was inside. And I was right."

"But I didn't kill him."

"Well, neither did I."

"You're right," I said, clarity sinking into my thoughts.

"Who?" Weston and Kurt said at the same time

"Both of you," I said, then turned to Jake. "Neither of them killed him. No one did."

Jake gaped at me.

I was still trying to pull the pieces together, but they were all there, right in front of me.

"Kurt, do you have a tattoo on your wrist?" I asked.

"Yeah," he said. "It's from a long time ago."

"And you put something over the camera on the deck before you came into the house, right?"

He sighed. "Yeah."

"Weston, at the card table, you said Clancy was cold as ice when you fell on top of him, right?" I moved toward where Clancy's body had been.

Weston nodded. "He was very cold."

"But you saw Kurt here that night," I said.

"Yes," Weston confirmed.

"And how long were you here before Xander and I showed up?" I asked.

"Probably only five or ten minutes," Weston said.

"Right," I said. "When we first came in, you told us

someone had run out the sliding door. Kurt, you tripped, leaving a bloody handprint on the deck."

Kurt nodded.

"And took off in your car. Your white car. The car Xander and I saw pulling onto the highway that night," I said. "The same car I helped move items out of that will probably provide essential information to this case. I'd bet in the rental car you have a tackle box with only fishing line and lures, heavy paper just like the kind the notes were on, and the remnants of Clancy's cell phone."

The entire room listened intently. I was onto something. I knew it.

"Jake, how long did it take the police to find the camera covered?" I asked.

"At least an hour," Jake said. "Maybe closer to an hour and a half."

"Which would mean that Kurt was only in the house, at maximum, two hours," I said. "And if Clancy's body really was cold, that would mean he would have died much earlier. Possibly even right after he left the sliding door unlocked."

"But how do you know someone didn't murder him?" Renée asked.

"That's more of a suspicion," I said. "If I had to guess, Clancy came home drunk. He left the sliding door unlocked after the alarms went off, then went to the kitchen to get himself something to drink. But the ice maker was broken and spewed ice all over the floor. Now, you and I both know Clancy couldn't have gotten down to pick up the ice. He couldn't even tie his shoes, right?"

Renée nodded. "I told him to schedule a session with

you, but he didn't think there was anything wrong with him. Especially when he had me to tie his shoes for him."

"So he would have left the melted ice there until Jasmine came back from vacation."

"Probably," Renée said.

"But because he was drunk, and the floor is exceptionally slippery when wet, he likely slipped on the ice or the water the ice left behind, hit his head on the counter, and bled to death on the floor."

A tear trickled down Renée's cheek. "If only I hadn't abandoned him."

Weston wrapped an arm around her shoulders, but she pushed him off and reached for the paw print charm at her throat.

"When both Kurt and Weston slipped in the blood or tripped over Clancy, they made it look like there was a struggle."

Jake rocked back on his heels and considered my theory. "The coroner still hasn't gotten back to me with their findings, but when they do, they'll either confirm or refute your theory."

"I have a feeling they'll confirm it." I winked.

He smiled and nodded once. "I suppose everyone is free to go."

Kurt's head shot up.

"Except you," Jake said. "You were still breaking and entering."

As everyone started filing out, Kurt turned back to me and said, "Maybe when I get out of jail, I can take you on a proper date?"

I shook my head. "No thanks. I don't date criminals."

"Let's go," Jake said, pulling Kurt toward the door.

"What about you?" Weston said to Renée. "Will you let me take you on a proper date?"

Renée looked up into his eyes. "I'm sorry, but no. At least, not right now."

"Timing is never on our side, is it?" Weston said with a laugh. "I'll see you in the field this spring."

She watched him leave and turned back to me. "Thank you so much. If it wasn't for you, we might never have known what really happened to Clancy."

"They still have to confirm my theory with the coroner," I said. "What are you going to do about all the people Clancy blackmailed? I'm sure they'll sue you once they find out you have their money."

"I'll leave that in my attorney's hands," she said. "Clancy may have been a crook, but he was also an investor. I'm certain I'll have plenty left over after I pay them all back."

"Enough to keep the farm and visit Argentina?" I asked.

"Enough to keep the farm and buy a place in Argentina." She laughed. "And speaking of Argentina . . ."

"Don't worry. We'll get you in tip-top shape so you can take that trip all by yourself."

"Yes, that would be good," she said. "But what if I don't want to go alone anymore?"

"I'm sure Weston would jump at the chance to go with you."

"Weston is not exactly who I was thinking of taking." She smiled at me.

"You want to take me? To Argentina?"

"Only if you teach me to tango," she said.

I was speechless.

"Is that a yes? I'll pay for everything. You don't have to worry about the money. And I'm sure someone can watch Penelope for you. Just please say yes."

"Yes," I said. "I'd love to go to Argentina with you."

She smiled and pulled me in for a hug. "Thank you for everything."

That evening, I had a new client to meet. Cliff Haven's only assisted living facility was north of town. You'd miss it if you didn't know it was there. The gates were old but kept in nice condition, and the driveway wound through a couple of hills to reveal a beautiful old home surrounded by small, newer cottages.

I checked in at the front desk. "I'm here to see Lucinda Blake."

"And you are?" The woman was formidable in stature but had a sweet smile.

"Ellie Vanderwick," I said. "I have a business called Relief with Ellie. Miss Blake's granddaughter asked me to stop by."

"Ah yes," the woman said. "I have a note about it right here."

She gave me a visitor badge on a lanyard to wear around my neck.

"If you could follow me, please?"

"Before we go, I'd like to make a donation." I pulled a

check out of my satchel and handed it to her. It hadn't taken long to decide what to do with my casino winnings.

Her eyes looked like they might pop out of her head when she saw the number. "This is very generous of you."

She pushed a few buttons on the computer and slipped the check into a safe, making sure it was locked afterward.

As she led me down the corridor of the old house, a feeling of warmth washed over me. The tickle in my scalp told me my hair was changing under my wide headband— probably turning a shade of pink.

A small voice sang a song on the other side of a pretty white door when the woman knocked. "Miss Blake? Ellie Vanderwick is here to see you."

The door opened gently, revealing a woman probably no taller than five foot two with long white hair wearing a pretty blue dress. "You're here to help me tie my shoes, right?" Her brownish-green eyes sparkled.

The woman from the front desk laughed as if she was joking, but I nodded. "That's exactly right."

"I'll leave you to it," the woman said, closing the door behind her.

"Miss Blake, I'm so happy to be here," I said.

"No, no, sweetheart, please call me Lucy." She handed me a pair of shoes with laces. "I'm thrilled you're here."

I was on a high from spending so much time with Lucy. Even after she'd gotten shoe tying down to an art, I still found myself visiting a couple times a week just to chat.

Something about her felt familiar, even though I was certain I'd never met her before.

Earlier that day, I'd gone to see her one last time before heading to the airport with Renée. She'd given me a big hug and made me promise to visit the moment I returned. Of course, I'd had no problem doing so.

When we got to the airport, it was packed with travelers, but Renée maneuvered around them like a pro. When we got to the baggage check, she lifted her suitcase onto the scale without so much as a grunt.

"That wasn't so hard," she said as we headed toward the security line.

"The true test is to come," I said.

She gave me a determined look. "I can do it."

As we waited for our turn to go through the metal detectors, my phone buzzed.

The sight of Xander's name on the screen instantly had me worried. He had agreed to watch Penelope while I was gone. Bex would have, but her dog didn't much like other animals.

I opened the text, dreading what he was about to tell me.

But relief replaced the worry when a photo popped up on the screen. Xander and Penelope's faces were squished together for the most adorable selfie I'd ever seen.

"That man is candy for the eyes," Renée said, peeking over my shoulder. "Why aren't the two of you together?"

"He's dating someone."

When I'd asked him to watch Penelope, he asked if Laura could hang out with them while I was gone. At my house.

He laughed when I told him no sleepovers, then assured me they were nowhere near that stage in their relationship.

"Too bad for her," Renée said, lifting her purse and small bag onto the conveyor belt.

"Why do you say that?"

"Because he obviously has feelings for someone else." She winked.

"We're just friends." I put my own satchel and bag on the conveyor belt along with my shoes and phone.

She shrugged. "Sometimes friends become more."

I hadn't let my mind wander to that place in several weeks. I'd been too busy trying—and failing—to locate my mother. Now, every time I tried, it was like my magic was absorbed into the dark recesses of my mind.

It wasn't that my magic wasn't working. It was. I'd even gotten my pillow to levitate for a few seconds.

But when it came to my mother, there was some sort of block. Like baking soda clearing odors in the refrigerator, my magic simply evaporated in thin air.

And to make matters worse, Esme's study was also proving to be more of a challenge than I anticipated. Some of the books were in different languages, but some wouldn't open at all.

Needless to say, I needed this vacation.

We had just enough time to grab a coffee before our plane started boarding.

"It's go time," Renée said as we handed the airline staff our tickets.

She marched down the boarding bridge with her shoulders back and her head held high.

"This is us," I said when we arrived at our seats. I popped the overhead compartment door open.

"Can I help you with that?" A young man asked Renée, noticing her bag and the empty compartment.

"I think I can get it," Renée said.

I smiled at him and mouthed, "Thanks."

Renée grabbed the bag with both hands, squatted down, then started lifting.

It was as if time was in slow motion.

She got the bag to her waist. Her chest.

Now was the hard part—getting it above her shoulders.

She'd done it in practice, but could she do it here?

If she couldn't, the trip would be a failure before we even left the airport.

With the bag past her shoulders, she pushed up onto her tiptoes and slid it securely inside the compartment.

She turned to me, and we both let out a triumphant yell causing all of the passengers to turn and face us.

Then the man who had offered his help started a slow clap and, before we knew it, everyone around us clapped along with him.

Renée wrapped me in a big hug. "Thank you, Ellie."

I laughed. "The trip has only just begun."

Thank you so much for reading *Tango Trouble*!

Don't miss Ellie's next adventure *Spelunking Speculation*! And while you wait, see what happens when Renée and Ellie encounter a mystery on their vacation in the FREE short story, *Argentina Alibi*.

If you enjoyed *Tango Trouble* and want to leave a review on Amazon or Goodreads, that would be amazing! Reviews help other readers choose which books to spend their time reading! You can also tell your friends about it too!

Also, I love hearing from readers! Email me at stellabixbyauthor@gmail.com.

XOXO,

Stella Bixby

ACKNOWLEDGMENTS

I'm learning, when you publish books this frequently, you end up thanking most of the same people over and over again.

I've also learned that as my book count increases, my amount of gratitude does as well.

Thank you to my friends and family for your constant love, support, patience, and willingness to let me vent about my never-ending book problems.

Thank you to all of my readers who email, comment, and message letting me know you enjoy my books.

Thank you to my beta readers who have had a HEAFTY work load this year so far. You are rockstars!

Thank you to my ARC team. Your reviews keep me going. Without your kind and honest feedback (and occasional typo help), writing would not be the joy that it is.

And last, but never least, thank You, God. Your love in my heart makes me want to spread joy through my words.

ABOUT THE AUTHOR

Stella Bixby is a native Coloradan who loves to snowboard, pluck at the guitar, and play board games with her family. She was once a volunteer firefighter and a park ranger, but now spends most of her time making up stories and trying to figure out what to cook for dinner.

Connect with Stella on Facebook, Twitter, and Instagram @StellaBixby.

Stella loves to hear from her readers!
www.stellabixby.com